THE ITALIAN AFFAIR

Recent Titles by Julie Ellis from Severn House

AVENGED

DEADLY OBSESSION

GENEVA RENDEZVOUS

NINE DAYS TO KILL

NO GREATER LOVE

SECOND TIME AROUND

VANISHED

THE
ITALIAN AFFAIR

Julie Ellis

This title first published in Great Britain 1998 by
SEVERN HOUSE PUBLISHERS LTD of
9–15 High Street, Sutton, Surrey SM1 1DF.
This title first published in the USA 1998 by
SEVERN HOUSE PUBLISHERS INC., of
595 Madison Avenue, New York, NY 10022.

British Library Cataloguing in Publication Data

Ellis,   Julie,   1933-
        The Italian Affair
        1.   Missing persons - Investigation - Italy - Fiction
        2.   Romantic suspense novels
        1. Title
        813.5'4 [F]

        ISBN 0-7278-5348-1

Printed and bound in Great Britain by
MPG Books Ltd, Bodmin, Cornwall.

ONE

Lisa Kirby—young, attractive, becomingly garbed in a sunlight-yellow silk suit that was smart but bought off a rack—leaned back in her plane seat and checked her watch. Twenty minutes out of International Airport, and the weather so perfect Lisa was scarcely aware of being airborne. The memory of recent events, while still painful, was already being overshadowed by the anticipation of what lay ahead. Before the hands of her watch could make a full sweep she would be in Milan.

Milano, her mother used to call the Italian city, Lisa recalled with a pang of nostalgia. Her mother had been an army nurse in Italy during World War II. Before the war was over, Lisa was born. A swift war romance and marriage. That was what Lisa had always thought, never questioned. Now the neat little pattern of the past had been thrown into chaos. In Milan, perhaps, she would find some answers to the multitude of questions that plagued her. She had to know.

That she could feel this strange stimulation at all, this sense of a whole new world about to open up before her, seemed odd to her. It was hard to believe that these last two nightmarish months were over; hard to believe that it had all even happened. . . .

The car accident that never should have happened! Her mother, strolling leisurely across Fifty-ninth

5

Street on a glorious spring day . . . keeping up a long-time romance with Central Park. . . . Her mother's favorite time of the year, when the earth threw off its winter coat, sending forth harbingers of summer. . . . And then, out of nowhere, the unexpected . . . a car out of control, mounting the sidewalk, spreading panic and tragedy. Stealing her mother's life away, except for those few, final, shock-filled hours.

Her mother had been young, Lisa remembered with renewed frustration. Forty-three, and still beautiful. And now she lay forever silent. Lisa shut her eyes, reliving again with tormenting clarity those last few minutes in a hospital room already cloaked with death.

Her mother lay back against the white hospital pillow, the white hospital sheets. The blinds drawn against the late afternoon sun that she would never see again. Lisa stood beside the high bed, one slender hand clutched between her own. Fighting against accepting reality.

"You must . . . you must go," her mother had reiterated with anguished urgency. ". . . Milano . . . Villa   Como . . . Remember . . . Villa Como!"

"Mom, please," Lisa entreated, the knot tightening in her throat.

Eloise Kirby's voice was a strained whisper, yet she was determined to speak. "Villa Como . . . for a summer of painting, Lisa—that's what you're to say. . . . They won't know Lisa Kirby . . . don't tell about your mother—" She tried to smile, struggling for strength to continue.

"Mom, don't talk," Lisa pleaded, clutching tensely at the hand between hers. Tears blotched the creaminess of her skin that was such a perfect foil for the midnight hair, the Italian-sky blueness of her eyes. "Darling, save your strength."

The doctors and nurses had left them alone at her mother's request. Nobody had to tell Lisa their time was brief.

The voice grew weaker but Eloise persisted. "Listen to me . . . money enough for a summer at the Villa . . . paying guest . . . in box at the bank —bonds, locket . . . Lisa, wear the locket always. . . . Be careful, darling . . . danger . . . much danger—" Lisa had to lean close to catch her mother's final words. "Find your brother, Lisa! . . . Find what belongs to you—"

"Mom!" The word was wrenched from her throat. Her eyes darkened, with fear as the cry went unheard. "Oh, Mom—"

Eloise Kirby's eyes were closed. The delicately chiseled face was relaxed, almost happy. Lisa lowered herself into the chair beside the narrow hospital bed and tried to make sense of her mother's dying, barely coherent plea.

Go to the Villa Como . . . find her brother? What brother? All her life, except for those first early years, there had been only her mother and herself. Now a brother? A tumultuous excitement tore at her in the midst of grief. A brother . . . and what else awaited her at the Villa Como? What was there at the Villa, where her mother had lived for a few war-ravaged weeks many years ago, that belonged to Lisa Kirby?

A few days later, Lisa sat alone in the apartment she had shared with her mother high above West Fifty-ninth Street. Impossible to stay on here, she decided with a shudder. She would have to sublet. The once warm and charming apartment, lovingly furnished through the years, was cold now, laden with ghosts.

Lisa forced herself to look at the manila envelope on the coffee table before her. The day after the funeral, she had compelled herself to go to the bank, to its cellar vaults, to ask for the bank box registered jointly in her mother's name and hers. Without looking at the box's contents in the privacy of the cubicle provided for such purposes, she dumped the miscellaneous papers, envelopes into the large, heavy manila envelope.

Lisa sighed in anguish. Each item in that manila envelope must now be carefully perused. She reached, undid the string, dumped the contents onto the table. Family papers, as she had expected. Birth certificates, marriage license, army discharge, bonds.

Lisa frowned, trying to concentrate on the task at hand. She skimmed each paper, noting dates from the past. And suddenly dates were not jibing with her memory. Here were indisputable facts—and yet. . . . Lisa reread. Her mother had been discharged from service in January of 1945. In May, 1945 Lisa was born. But the marriage supposedly performed in March of the previous year took place two months before Lisa's birth!

Lisa tried to bring into sharper focus the shadowy memory of her father. A tall, good-humored man who laughed a lot . . . tossing her in the air until she squealed with delight. Memories of herself walking between her mother and that man, secure in belonging, in being loved.

She was four when he died of pneumonia. Who was her real father? Certainly not the man who had married her mother, seven months pregnant. Then was her father still alive—living somewhere in Milan? And her brother? What of him? And why had her mother said, "Find your brother"? Why not, "Find your father"? Because her father must be dead, Lisa recognized with a fleeting, poignant regret.

Lisa lifted the small, velvet covered jewelry box from the table, pried it open. The locket was there. How exquisite! A beautifully tooled, antique gold medallion on a slender chain. Lisa held the locket in one hand, inspecting the delicate imagery. A man and a woman in close embrace. She turned it over. A quotation, in Italian, from Dante.

In April her mother had died; now it was the end of May and Lisa was bound for Milan. How fortunate that her mother had insisted on her studying Italian. Instinct warned her that it would be to her advantage to keep secret the extent of this ability.

Her office had insisted that she take leave, rather than resign. But Lisa was sure, deep within, that she would never return to the drafting board in her old office. She was two weeks past twenty. To the rebelliousness and impatience of youth was added a furious desire to discover the truth about her origins. To disinter the secret of the Villa Como.

It had been astonishingly simple, despite her first apprehensions, to inquire and learn about various summer accommodations available in the vicinity of

Milan. Among the recommended villas taking in paying guests had been the Villa Como. She received a polite letter from the Signora Pia Menotti welcoming her as a guest on behalf of herself and the Contessa. A definite date of arrival had been designated, with a subtle arrogance that annoyed Lisa's American independence. They were not too arrogant to accept American dollars, this Contessa and her daughter-in-law, who called herself the manageress of the Villa Como's paying guest wing. There would be only four guests besides herself, Lisa had been informed.

Lisa closed her eyes. The last few weeks had been exhausting. An uneasy fear stirred within her despite the sense of adventure as she contemplated the summer ahead. In a way she was grateful for the need to think beyond herself, to shunt grief aside for the search that lay before her. Danger, her mother had warned. And her mother had been a courageous woman, not prone to unwarranted fear or exaggerations. Lisa was the tempestuous, highly imaginative member of the family. What was her brother like? Her excitement rose as she contemplated a family heretofore unknown. Her mother had been marvelously alive, warm, close to her. It was frightening to be alone in a world of strangers. With luck—keeping clear of the danger her mother had cautioned against—she might not be alone.

Lisa stood in the milling crowd at the Milan airport, relieved to be through customs. She had been met at the airport barrier on schedule by Pia Menotti, who issued orders in swift Italian to a porter hovering near. Pia turned now to query a man behind a small

kiosk on their left. As she asked him about the incoming plane from London, its arrival was announced via the loudspeaker.

"Grazie." Pia's smile for the man behind the kiosk
was condescending. Nevertheless, the man obviously
admired both Pia and her paying guest.

Lisa guessed that Pia Menotti was no more than
an inch taller than her own five feet four inches. But
Pia had a way of carrying her full-blown figure that
added inches to her stature. She had a fine head and
Madonna-like hair, and she would have been a
beautiful woman, the artist in Lisa conceded, except
for the dissatisfaction that lurked in the somber dark
eyes, detracting from true beauty.

Incoming crowds jostled about them and collided
with the outgoing travelers amid much noisy conversation, high spirits, and occasional indignation
elicited from touchy, thin-skinned passengers as luggage inadvertently tangled with bodies. Lisa noticed
many Americans her own age, the college cliques out
to see Europe, calm English families and the more
volatile Italians, French and Spanish. Vacation time
in full force, she realized for the first time. She had
been living inwardly too much these last few weeks
to be aware of the world around her.

"We wait for Signor Anderson," Pia Menotti broke
into Lisa's introspection with a sort of reluctant
cordiality, speaking in a self-conscious but fluid English. "His plane has arrived."

"It was kind of you to drive all the way in from the
villa," Lisa said, recalling that a girl at the travel
agency had mentioned the availability of buses passing
close to the Villa Como.

"We prefer to have our guests comfortable." Pia smiled impersonally. "It's only a bit more than twenty kilometers to the villa. We drive it in forty minutes at the most." Pia shrugged, her eyes traveling about the crowds searching for her second passenger. "Signor Anderson is a writer, American, like you," Pia said with a note of condescension that annoyed Lisa. "The other guests are three English school teachers on sabbatical."

If Pia Menotti resented the intrusion, why bother, Lisa asked herself with smoldering antagonism; but the explanation was simple. Money. Lisa's mind tabulated the facts. Pia Menotti, *Signora* Menotti, was the daughter-in-law of the contessa. Both the contessa and Pia Menotti were widows; this had been elaborately explained in the correspondence, as though to say that the lack of men in their lives accounted for the opening up of the villa to strangers. Who, then, was the man presumably her brother? Lisa harbored no doubts of her mother's lucidity in those painful, final moments. Her mother *knew*. For some reason all these years, she had remained silent about the secret of the Villa Como, but her mother knew.

"That must be Signor Anderson," Pia said suddenly, a different quality in her voice. A feminine appraisal that held approval. It was at the same time a guarded quality, Lisa noted. Pia moved to the left a couple of feet, planting herself squarely in front of the small kiosk. A designated meeting place.

Lisa's glance followed Pia's, coming to rest on a tall, sandy-haired, broad-shouldered man with an air of authority about him. Handsome in a rugged yet clean-cut fashion that suggested strength.

"How do you know that's Anderson?" Lisa asked curiously, absorbed in her own scrutiny, yet strangely glad that this man would be a fellow guest in the crucial weeks that lay ahead of her.

"He is an American," Pia said with an inscrutable smile. "The clothes."

His business suit would have been indistinguishable from hundreds of others along Madison Avenue, but here in the Milan waiting room it marked him, Lisa realized. The shoes, comfortable loafers, indicated an independent mind, she decided, liking this divergence from the typical. In one hand he gripped the handle of a portable typewriter case, while under the other arm he struggled with a pair of new, expensive leather valises. Pia Menotti had said he was a writer, and Lisa wondered what he wrote.

"Signora Menotti?" He came to a halt before them. His voice was deep, pleasantly warm. Lisa found herself gazing compulsively. "I'm Scott Anderson."

"I am Pia Menotti," she acknowledged coolly.

The porter who had spirited away Lisa's luggage hovered near, and Pia gestured to him to relieve Scott Anderson, who insisted on hanging on to the portable typewriter himself.

"Superstitious about this thing," he grinned disarmingly, including Lisa in the explanation, and instantly Pia introduced them.

Lisa felt herself grow warm with self-consciousness as she realized the intensity of her gaze upon Scott

Anderson. Pia Menotti, too, was taking candid inventory. Hazel eyes that would be almost black in excitement or anger, Lisa appraised, a strong jaw-line —stubborn, like herself. A man richly endowed with charm. A man who knew much about women. Young, twenty-eight or thirty. Already, Pia Menotti was reacting with a fresh awareness of herself as a woman. Lisa felt a bit of satisfaction that being a fellow American lent them a kinship, and was glad.

In a matter of minutes the porter had stowed his luggage away beside hers in the trunk of Pia Menotti's black Mercedes, and they were settled in the car, Scott and Lisa in the rear, Pia behind the wheel. Scott had just arrived from London, where he had been for the past five weeks on business, he explained in detail. Before London, he had been in Mexico for a year.

The reference to Mexico sent Lisa into the past. The summer before, she had toured Mexico with her mother for six weeks. She retreated into a silence that Scott Anderson went to great lengths to pierce, but without success. He at last acknowledged defeat, settling for small talk with Pia Menotti about Europe in general.

In the Italian summer twilight, Pia Menotti drove with an unrelenting speed around the curved roads, though she drove with skill, along roads she obviously knew well. The city disappeared behind them. Gradually, Lisa found herself concentrating on the beauty of the countryside. There were olive groves along one side of the road as they approached their destination. The cypress on the other side lent a pleasantly pungent scent to the warm air of the early evening.

"The villa is right ahead," Pia announced with pride. "We live now in the wing to the right. The left wing is closed. Here, too, we have a servant problem."

"Should be a great place to work," Scott Anderson decided with satisfaction, focusing again on Lisa.

"I think so," Lisa conceded, breaking through her shell of silence. "I'm looking forward to it."

"Artist?" he questioned, one eyebrow lifted in good-humored curiosity.

"Trying to be," Lisa said self-consciously. "I promised myself a summer of painting to find out."

"Many people come here to paint," Pia injected. "There is a very elusive beauty about the villa that they try to capture."

Pia slowed down as they approached massive wrought-iron gates, which were open to receive them.

She drove through, came to a stop, then announced: "I will lock the gates." She pushed open the car door. "We are all in for the night. If you wish to leave in the evenings, please advice the contessa or myself."

A chill settled about Lisa as she watched Pia guide the heavy gates into their locked position. She fought down an incipient panic. All at once night was closing in about them, and now the locked gates. She was aware that Scott Anderson was scrutinizing her, and she flushed self-consciously.

"These trees are beautifully old, aren't they? Ever smell a fireplace burning olive branches?" He sniffed eagerly. "There," he decided in triumph. "That marvelous smell! Somebody has a fire laid up there in the villa."

Scott was conscious of her unease, Lisa guessed, and she tried to divert her thoughts. Her mother would have liked Scott Anderson, she decided impulsively, fresh confidence flowing within her again. You never felt completely alone in a foreign country as long as there was a friendly fellow American close by.

"Tomorrow, you will see the lemon terraces and the lake," Pia said, sliding behind the wheel again. "The gardens are particularly beautiful this time of year." She spoke absently, as though reciting a speech. "Wisteria vines that have been growing for generations. Begonias, hydrangeas, azaleas. Many artists enjoy painting our gardens."

The black Mercedes crawled up the incline approaching the villa. It was a massive structure, ornate and impressive. The car stopped before a sprawling terrace. Before they emerged from the car, a door on the terrace opened, and in the shadowed light from within they saw the woman standing there. Small of stature, almost tiny, but with a bearing similar to Pia's. A woman brimming over with pride, arrogance, Lisa guessed. Once, years ago, she must have been beautiful, in the manner of northern Italians with their blue eyes and fair hair. Now the hair was gray, and the eyes were scornful, bitter. The contessa.

Pia preceded them up the stairs to the terrace, spoke in low, swift Italian to the woman at the door. In their correspondence it had been established that both Pia Menotti and the contessa spoke English fluently, that the language barrier would offer no problems. Lisa reminded herself to continue the assumption that her own Italian was limited.

"Welcome to our villa," the contessa greeted them with a condescending cordiality that mirrored her daughter-in-law's. "I am the contessa, your hostess. I trust your trip was pleasant?"

"Very," Lisa said quietly. Scott had gone back to the Mercedes, remembering the luggage, insistent that Pia leave this to him. "I've been looking forward so to my visit here." No gushing, Lisa warned herself, but eagerness. Play the part well!

"Pia will show you your rooms," the contessa continued, ushering Lisa inside. "Rosa has prepared a light supper when you have refreshed yourselves and are ready."

"How beautiful," Lisa said with involuntary awe as she walked with the contessa into the marble-floored foyer with its high circular staircase and exquisite chandelier. Tapestries lined the wall along the staircase, not quite concealing the fact that these areas had once been covered by something else.

"There was a time, before the war," the contessa said, bitterness darkening the still beautiful blue eyes, "when this wall was an art gallery of priceless treasures. There are two paintings yet remaining, that the Fascists were unable to discover. At the top of the stairs you will see. There is another in my personal sitting room." Now the contessa cautiously scrutinized Lisa. "You are the artist, yes?"

"Trying to be," Lisa amended, straining to catch the conversation between Pia and Scott Anderson directly behind her.

"Signor Anderson is a writer," Pia brought them into the conversation. There was an odd warning in her eyes as they met the contessa's. Yet Lisa sensed the warning had nothing to do with Scott. In some way it was directed towards her. Why? "Miss Kirby, do you speak French?" Pia asked with a velvet swiftness, calculated, Lisa felt, to trap her.

"Not a bit," Lisa said without hesitancy, again intercepting an exchange between the contessa and Lisa. Her answer seemed to please them. "I'm afraid I'm a typical American," Lisa laughed in casual apology. "Except for a dozen words of Italian, I speak only my own language."

The contessa directed her attention now to Scott Anderson. "It will be a pleasure to have a man in the villa again." From the blend of speculation and warmth in the contessa's eyes, Lisa guessed the contessa must have been, in her younger days, a woman with an eye for attractive men. "We are, except for yourself, a household of women."

"The pleasure is mine," Scott murmured, eyes opaque after a momentary exchange with Pia's that was hotly personal.

Lisa's heart pounded as she considered the lie behind the contessa's statement that this was a maleless household. There *was* a man somewhere in the Villa Como—and that man was her brother.

"Pia, you will please show our guests to their rooms." The contessa was dismissing them, politely but definitely. "I will tell Rosa to be in readiness."

"The guest list is small, I gather," Scott remarked

to Pia as the three ascended the wide marble staircase.

Pia nodded. "Miss Kirby, yourself, and three English ladies. The English are school teachers on sabbatical, who use the villa as their base. They spend much time touring about the countryside." Pia's voice was a model of politeness, but her eyes, when they lingered on Scott, smoldered. She walked with a deliberate swing of the hips that was meant to emphasize the provocative curves of her torso beneath a deceptively simple white linen sheath.

"What lovely tapestries," Lisa murmured in deep respect, eyes skimming the dimly lit staircase wall.

"Fourteenth century, probably," Scott Anderson conjectured with admiration. "Magnificent."

"We believe fourteenth century," Pia concurred, a note of surprise in her voice, as though not quite believing that an American could be so cognizant of Italian treasures.

"I did some research on tapestries for an article some years ago," he said, almost too quickly.

Why should he be annoyed at himself for knowing about fourteenth century tapestries, Lisa wondered.

It was as if one had moved back centuries into an age of old world charm just to walk into a house like this, Lisa thought. Her mother might have walked this same staircase, felt this same reverence for the beauty of the surroundings. It seemed strange that her mother, who was so vocal about everything, had been so vague about the name of the villa until those last few moments in the hospital. They were at the landing now, where the carpeting was worn.

Pia stopped before a heavy oak door. "This will be your room, Miss Kirby." For a moment Pia Menotti's dark eyes swept over the willowy figure in the sunlight yellow suit, as though taking inventory. There was a certain arrogance in the glance that expressed pride in the full-blown voluptuousness of her own figure. "I hope you will find it pleasant." Pia dug into an oversized pocket to produce keys, and Lisa caught sight of the tin of English pipe tobacco tucked away in the same pocket. "When you are ready for supper, Miss Kirby, please join us below."

Pia swung open the door. With a conspiratorial grin Scott walked inside, deposited the one valise belonging to Lisa that Pia had permitted him to carry up from the car. The servants would transport the others, they had been informed.

"I hope this is the right one," he chuckled, his eyes for a moment holding Lisa's, oddly reassuring her.

"It is," Lisa said with a smile. She was glad Scott Anderson and she had arrived together.

Scott glanced about the room with leisurely interest. "I've lived in apartments that were smaller than this." He smiled in approval.

"In Paris?" Pia queried. "Many old villas there have been converted into flats, of course."

"In New York," he corrected. "I don't know much about Paris. Changed planes there once."

"It's a beautiful room," Lisa said, discomforted by the exchange between Scott and Pia that seemed to shut her out. Lisa became aware of a hostility rising in her towards the tall, dark-haired Pia.

Excitement welled in Lisa as she surveyed the huge room with its enormous, heavily draped windows, its

blend of fine old furniture and antiquish mail-order
pieces. But the high, polished bed was genuine, Lisa
decided with satisfaction, inspecting the sheen of the
old wood. Enormous pillows and a comforter were
placed across the foot in readiness for the coolness of
an Italian evening. This was a country of high winds,
Lisa remembered. When she was a child, winds in
the night used to terrify her. Nostalgia touched her
with painful sharpness as she remembered nights
when she cuddled in her mother's arms, when winds
howled high above the city and rain lashed at their
windows.

"I will show you your room, Signor Anderson,"
Pia said brusquely.

The heavy door swung shut behind Pia and Scott.
Again Lisa experienced a feeling of being closed in,
beyond escape. She stood motionless, ears straining to
hear the sounds in the hallway—a door opening in
the next room; footsteps over the thick carpeting,
muted but distinct. Scott Anderson would be in the
room next door. Relief flooded her.

Deeply conscious of the newness of her surroundings, Lisa shed her jacket, hesitated a moment, then
stepped from the skirt, pulled off her blouse. An open
door led to the dressing room, which had ample closet
space, a massive chest, a large oval mirror, and a
couch—where no doubt some earlier guests had
bedded down a child during their visit.

Lisa walked into the bathroom. Ornate, almost
baroque. Large, in keeping with the size of the bedroom. A scent of a heavy French perfume lingered.
The plumbing was more modern than Lisa would
have expected. With a determination not to be caught

up in morbid introspection, she went about the routine of applying fresh make-up. After all, Pia Menotti was a strikingly attractive woman. Pride insisted that Lisa not fade into Pia's shadow.

Lisa inspected herself, frowning at the faint shadows still lingering beneath her eyes. She had not been sleeping well since her mother's tragic accident. Strangely, she had the feeling that tonight, with Scott Anderson in the room next door, she would sleep.

She returned to the bedroom. Its shadowed lighting seemed in harmony with the villa—and helped keep Villa Como bills to a minimum, she thought with a glimmer of humor as she hoisted the valise to the bed. A turquoise summer knit lay in readiness. She pulled down the zipper, slid the silken softness over her head, down about her slender, supple dimensions. The turquoise was flattering, she decided with pleasure.

In the next room Scott whistled as he moved about. Then he obviously settled down to make notes because the typewriter keys pierced the silence with determined regularity. Something about the click of the typewriter keys puzzled her. What? Nonsense, Lisa chided herself. She was so pent up that everything not instantly recognizable was suspect.

Lisa frowned with indecision as she hovered over the valise. Her mother had said, "Wear the locket always." No need for delay. She dug beneath the soft pile of clothing, found the box, brought it out. She was here for a purpose. The medallion was in her hands now, and Lisa commanded herself to be realistic. Strange that her mother referred to this as a locket, this heavy slab of antique gold on a chain.

There was no opening for a locket, only the exquisitely tooled figures of a man and a woman in embrace.

Lisa locked the chain about her neck, took a final, anxious glance at herself in the mirror above the dresser. All right, downstairs now for the supper that was being prepared. She was aware, all at once, that the typewriter next door was silent.

As though prearranged, Scott and she emerged simultaneously from their rooms. His smile was warm, encouraging, as if he sensed that she felt insecure, self-conscious about taking up living in this foreign villa.

"I don't know about you, Lisa Kirby," he smiled as he fell into step beside her, "but I'm absolutely famished."

"Between us we'll probably shock the daylights out of the Menottis." Her eyes met his with a hint of laughter. "There's nothing delicate about my appetite."

Some of the tensions began to ease away from Lisa. At the moment they were two young people, pleasantly aware of each other. She was glad Scott Anderson was here in the villa. She decided with a surge of optimism that whatever happened, she could depend upon him to help.

Scott stopped at the head of the marble staircase and leaned forward intently. "Say, I didn't get a real look at this before." A fresh excitement laced his voice as he inspected the handsomely framed painting that adorned the wall.

"A light bulb must have just been replaced," Lisa noted, moving forward to view the painting.

"It's fabulous," Scott exclaimed, squinting in concentration.

"I'm awe-stricken," Lisa said. Imagine living in a villa where a Modigliani hung on the wall!

"It's absolutely the finest reproduction I've ever encountered," Scott acknowledged, and Lisa turned to him in shock. She had accepted it as an original. "The oils aged to match, everything just right. Modigliani himself might have had to look twice to be sure."

Lisa's eyes widened in astonishment. "Are you an artist?" Only an artist could have possibly noticed the pigments. An artist of experience, discernment.

"Hardly," Scott scoffed, too swiftly for credibility. Trying for a laugh.

Why did he lie this way, Lisa asked herself in towering curiosity?

"Writing's my job," he said. "I'm adding one and one and getting four. A family taking in paying guests would hardly own an authentic Modigliani."

"I suppose not," Lisa admitted self-consciously. He made his reasoning sound logical enough, yet she wasn't buying.

He put a hand at her elbow. "Let's go down there and polish off that fine Italian supper I'll wager is waiting for us. Probably a feast."

Lisa recalled her mother's warning. "Danger. Much danger." What was the danger? In a villa where a fellow American posed as a writer, even to pecking away at a typewriter key to carry along the deception. That was what had bugged her earlier! Scott Anderson had *not* been typing. He had been hammering away at one key, to create the illusion that he was typing. For her benefit? To convince the Menottis that he was something he was not? Why was it so urgent that nobody at the Villa Como should realize Scott Anderson was an artist? And this was the man she had so naively decided was a hold on safety!

What about Pia Menotti? And the contessa, who had made such a point of claiming the villa was male-less? With the exception of Scott Anderson, of course. Pia Menotti had brought back a tin of English pipe tobacco from Milan. Certainly not for her consumption, nor the contessa's. Even the servants were supposedly female.

Lisa's head whirled with questions, apprehensions, doubts. Who at the Villa Como would provide her with answers?

TWO

Lisa awoke slowly, cautiously, aware of the faint inner excitement that accompanies a realization of being in unfamiliar surroundings. She pushed back the satin comforter. The room had become warm with summer heat. Perspiration moistened her forehead.

She maneuvered the pair of enormous pillows against the headboard and settled into their downy softness. Blue eyes, still mildly sleep-logged, surveyed the shadowed room in approval. Absolutely

Edwardian in size, she decided, feeling herself enveloped in luxury.

Still quite early, Lisa guessed, her gaze settling on the heavy brocades at the windows, which blocked out any vestige of morning light. An urge to see beyond the cloistered windows propelled her to her feet. She walked barefoot across the thick green carpeting to a window and pushed aside the blue silk brocade drapes, the cascade of sheer white curtains, bringing filtered sunlight into the room. No wonder she was so warm, Lisa realized; the windows were closed tight, as well as the shutters.

She leaned forward, caught her breath at the beauty of the view that lay outside. Last night, in the dark, in the flurry of arrival, she had forgot that the Villa was beside a lake. The sun was a red-orange ball hanging in the early morning light-blue Italian sky, its color delicately reflected in the mist rising above the water. The mountains beyond, snow-capped even in June, were an awesome background for the glory of the lake.

Oh, to put this on canvas, Lisa mused with a sense of pleasure; to preserve this moment of exquisite discovery. It was as if her mother were standing here beside Lisa, pointing out highlights of the country. Lisa stood motionless, wishing with nostalgia that her mother and she had come to the Villa Como together.

In the distance church bells rang. Her mother had spoken about the grandeur of the churches throughout Italy, the way even the poorest of villages contrived to maintain a place of worship that would have been at home in the wealthiest of towns. Above the sound of the church bells was the jarring intrusion of a steady hum of traffic. Italian cars, motor scooters, the buses that passed the Villa. The sounds were so incongruous to this ancient setting.

Lisa turned away from the window, eager to inspect her room in detail. Last night her impressions had been quickly garnered. Now she moved about the ivory-walled room and noted each piece of furniture: the ones she suspected were genuine, the obvious mail-order fill-ins, like the pseudo-Renaissance desk in the far corner of the room. There were highly polished, beautifully grained chairs, painstakingly recovered recently in a sophisticated modern blue. The chairs, Lisa decided, were authentic antiques, as was the fruitwood chest where she had deposited her watch the night before.

A marble fireplace lent an air of sybaritic luxury to the room, to Lisa's way of thinking. A fire was laid of piled-up olive branches which gave off a pungent scent she could not identify.

None of the rush of the old life back in New York, Lisa mused with satisfaction, crossing to the chest to consult her watch. Reaching for the watch, her eyes settled on the painting above the dresser. Excitement welled in her as she considered who the artist might be. The painting, a pastoral, was of the twentieth century, Lisa guessed, but the altar-like Gothic frame was a reproduction of one made in the fifteenth century.

Lisa picked up her watch. Not yet seven. She had adjusted her watch to Italian time; it was correct. What was she doing awake at so ungodly an hour? Only a month ago she would have been lying in bed, clutching at sleep. At eight, the very last possible moment on working mornings, she would unwind herself from the tangle of bedclothes, shower, dress, stop off for breakfast in the drugstore downstairs, and hurry into her office at the stroke of nine. No need to rush now. But Lisa felt that time was slipping through her fingers because she had learned nothing yet.

She was conscious of someone stirring in the next room. She was not the only early riser this morning. Scott's voice humming pleasantly was just audible through the thick walls. Pia Menotti had said breakfast would be served in the rooms. Not that their hostesses were so concerned for their comfort, Lisa guessed; rather, it forestalled the guests becoming active members of the household.

Lisa pulled a duster over her nightie, crossed to the windows with a determination to bring full morning sunlight into the room. She discovered with delight a minute balcony that opened up from what she had supposed to be just another window. She walked out to welcome the warm morning breeze.

"What are *you* doing up at the break of dawn?" a male voice chided with good-natured mockery. She swung about to face Scott Anderson, who leaned over a matching balcony. "If I were a romantic, I would slide down to the ground and quote from 'Romeo and Juliet'," he chuckled.

"It's ridiculous to be up so early, I suppose—but have you ever seen a day quite so beautiful?" Her enthusiasm surged to the surface.

"Wait till you see the lake in another two hours— real Italian postcard blue," Scott promised.

Scott waved to someone in the garden below, and Lisa followed his gaze. A young Italian girl scrubbed at the statuary set in the garden fountain. She waved back, giggled, gathered up her pail and scrubbing brush and disappeared in the thick summer foliage.

"You look young enough to be Juliet," Scott teased Lisa. "What are you doing all alone in Italy?"

"I'm twenty," Lisa flashed back. Scott was not more than eight or ten years older than she was, she decided defensively. "I don't travel with a nursemaid." His solicitous attitude annoyed her. "Will you excuse me?" she said haughtily. "I really must unpack."

Actually, she had unpacked the night before. Now she stalked back inside the room, her cheeks warm. He had not looked at Pia Menotti as if *she* were fourteen.

It was going to be a humid summer day. Lisa decided on shorts and a blouse, thonged sandals. She dressed, ran a brush expertly over her hair and stared at her reflection in a large ornate mirror. She reached for the locket and hesitated. It did not belong with the shorts and blouse. But Italians were noted for sentimentality, they would not think it unusual.

Lisa started at a light knock on the bedroom door. The girl in the garden must have reported that she was awake.

"Avanti," she called, then reminded herself that she was an American, who spoke no Italian. She bit her lip in annoyance. How easy it was to slip! Her life might depend upon such secrecy. "Good morning." She managed a bright, casual smile for the eager-eyed young Italian girl who carried a tray into the room. It was the girl she had seen in the garden a short while ago. Obviously, the girl approved of the American guests.

"Americano breakfast," the girl purred with sultry satisfaction, pointing to the platter of eggs, the pot of steaming coffee. "Rosa bake fresh rolls."

"It looks delicious," Lisa acknowledged, following the girl to the table and watching as the girl set it up before the balcony. Six months ago Lisa would have laughed in disbelief if someone had said that she would be sitting at a balcony in an Italian villa, having breakfast before a breathtaking expanse of blue lake and sky.

"*Molto bello*," the girl gestured extravagantly at the outdoors. "*Si?*" She pulled a chair deftly into position.

"*Si*," Lisa nodded enthusiastically, making a show of guessing at the words. The girl stared in candid interest at Lisa's smartly tailored blue blouse, matching shorts, the locket with its gold chain. For a moment, as the girl gazed intently at the locket, Lisa's pulse quickened. "*Molto bello*," the girl said politely. The locket meant nothing to her—he was too ingenuous to dissemble, Lisa realized. Just a momentary interest.

"What is your name?" Lisa asked. "You do speak English?"

"A leetle," the girl preened. "My name Maria."

"Thank you, Maria." The girl was only a year or two younger than she, Lisa guessed, but somehow she felt so worldly in comparison. It was a reassuring feeling.

Lisa lifted the table onto the tiny balcony, careful not to disturb the appealing breakfast. The way Scott and she had eaten last night, the Menottis must be convinced that they had gigantic appetites. Forcing herself not to look at the adjoining balcony, though her ears were cocked for the slightest sound, she dragged out the chair and seated herself in the June sunlight to gorge on Rosa's version of the perfect American breakfast—three eggs, warm rolls, strong, fragrant coffee.

Disappointment tugged at her. Scott was eating his breakfast indoors.

Lisa waited until almost ten to go downstairs. She could hear the contessa somewhere in the rear of the house, in sharp consultation with the cook, obviously out of sorts over some household misdemeanor.

Sunlight flowed into the rooms through now opened windows and shutters. The three English school teachers, Lisa remembered from last night's supper conversation, were off on a visit to Venice. They had rented a Fiat, Pia had confided, and for Scott's benefit, made a lively story of their leave-taking. Besides the servants, there were only the contessa, Pia Menotti, Scott and herself in the entire villa. Who would be the one to lead her to her brother, Lisa asked herself. Somewhere within this household was someone who knew the truth.

Easel under one arm, paints and brushes in the other, Lisa strolled from the house, across the wide terrace, down gently graded steps, and into the cypress-hedged gardens. Flowers grew in such abundance that Lisa stopped here and there to soak up their beauty and to listen to the exultant songs of the birds as they flitted from one perch to another.

She heard voices coming from the other side of a row of cypresses. She listened closely, trying to identify them. Soon the voices were loud enough for her to recognize them, though not close enough for her to hear the conversation. Scott and Pia.

Determined to be aloof, ashamed of the trickle of jealousy that flowed through her, Lisa looked resolutely about to find a corner in which to work, a corner that would be hers for six weeks. Again, something akin to panic touched her because six weeks was a frightening short span of time.

She set up her easel and sought to concentrate on the magnificence before her. She had deliberately sought out this view. From here she could see whoever arrived at the villa. Up that driveway must come a man who would be her brother. Possibly the man for whom Pia Menotti bought English smoking tobacco in Milan.

The voices were close now. Lisa, making sweeping strokes with the brush across her canvas, felt a little guilty about eavesdropping.

"Let's sit down a few moments," Scott suggested. "You're accustomed to all this. Let a view-hungry tourist enjoy it."

"You will not get much work done," Pia warned with throaty amusement. "Not if you are turning tourist."

"I owe myself a few days of loafing," Scott said undisturbed. "I work like a madman when I get down to it. Go on, tell me more about the Villa Como," he urged.

"I have carried you straight up from the fourteenth century," Pia pointed out. "You know as much about the villa as I do now."

Pia was a Menotti by marriage, Lisa reminded herself. Pia Menotti was a widow, but she hadn't elaborated on how she had become one. All Lisa knew was that Pia was the contessa's daughter-in-law and that Pia's husband—the contessa's son—was dead.

Pia was not the kind of woman to remain without a man, Lisa guessed. The tin of tobacco kept bothering her. Where was the man for whom it was intended?

"What about during the war years?" Scott asked Pia casually. "The villa seems to have survived well."

"That was before my time. I was a small child living then near Naples," Pia reminded. "The Fascists were here, though, and after them came the Americans." Her voice became harsh and bitter.

"Americans were billeted here?" Scott ignored the scorn in Pia's voice. She was an attractive woman. Typical male, Lisa thought.

"At one time a regiment of American women," Pia said with sardonic humor. "Can you not picture what it must have been like here?"

Lisa froze, her pulse hammering away in her throat. Her mother had been in that regiment of American women—WACS—billeted at the Villa Como.

"There are several versions," Scott teased. "Tough on your women, pleasant for your men."

"American women in uniform?" Pia jibed. "What Italian would succumb to something so unfeminine?"

But one had, Lisa remembered, excitement sending chills through her bloodstream. Her father! One of those Italian men.

"Of course, in those days," Pia continued, "the villa was not so sparsely occupied. "The Menotti men were all anti-Fascists, partisans. The villa was their haven. There were many caverns in which to hide. The old contessa, my husband's grandmother, died in a Fascist prison for her work with the underground."

"She must have been quite a lady," Scott said gently.

Lisa started at the sound of foliage being brushed aside. She swung about to face Rosa. The cook's dark eyes were somber, suspicious, despite the smile on her lined, multi-chinned face.

"Today is—", the old woman said, searching for the English word, "hot." She sighed with satisfaction. "I bring you *caffe.*" Rosa nodded towards the tray with the pitcher of ice coffee.

"*Grazie,*" Lisa smiled, eager to be friends with the old woman who had been with the family for many years. What had the contessa said at supper last night about Rosa being at the Villa Como before she herself? Perhaps Rosa had served Lisa's mother.

Rosa's eyes shot sidewards as she bent to deposit the tray on the ground. And with a look, almost venomous, she muttered an Italian epithet that cast aspersions on Pia's parentage. Rosa had come to the garden with iced coffee for Lisa in order to spy on Pia and Scott, Lisa guessed. She fought to conceal her astonishment. Beneath the outward serenity at the villa, Lisa sensed intrigue building. Obviously,

Rosa distrusted Pia, and Scott, because Pia was friendly with him. Why?

Now Rosa stalled, inspecting the random strokes on the canvas with a frenzied interest that elicited soft laughter from Lisa. She had seen that same intensity on faces at a Greenwich Village art show. Faces that were determined to find art in smudges offered for sale. Then Rosa frowned, her dark eyes darting towards the row of cypresses that made a screen between Lisa and the two on the other side.

"The village is quite charming," Pia said. Something in her voice indicated she was aware that she was being overheard. "You will find much of what I believe you call local color, in the shops around the Piazza."

"Perhaps I can persuade you to show me about," Scott suggested casually.

Typical American male in pursuit, Lisa thought in disdain. He had taken one look at this busty Italian babe and remembered all the earthy Italian movies he had seen! Couldn't the fool see in what contempt Pia Menotti held Americans? Or was she about to make an exception for a good-looking American male posing as a writer? It was impossible to hear Pia's response to Scott's suggestion. Pia had moved him beyond earshot.

"You live in Paris for while?" Rosa asked, garrulous now that the "manageress" had taken off. "You make paintings in Paris, yes?"

"No," Lisa said regretfully. "I've never been to Paris."

Why that lost, hopeless look on Rosa's face, Lisa

wondered. Certainly not because Rosa was an advocate of Paris study for artists. Why was Rosa so eager to believe that Lisa had arrived at the villa by way of Paris? Last night Pia had asked if she spoke French, and both Pia and the Contessa had appeared relieved when she admitted that she did not. High school French seemed hardly worthy of mention. Rosa smoothed the apron over her mountainous belly and stared at the ground. Then with another sigh, she waddled away, along a side path that Lisa had not noticed before. Lisa sensed that in some way she had deeply disappointed Rosa.

She tried with genuine sincerity to concentrate on a morning of painting, but the odds were stacked too heavily against her. First morning, Lisa thought, excusing herself. Scott had said that, too, she remembered with a flurry of hostility. She laid aside her brush and reached to pour icy coffee into a tall ruby glass. The glass appeared to be an heirloom. Probably bought at the Milan version of the five-and-ten, Lisa thought scornfully. The contessa would never allow heirloom glassware out in the garden for the use of American guests.

Lisa sipped slowly, enjoying the cool liquid. A breeze had drifted in from the west. She finished the drink, gazed about with a feeling of being at loose ends. Why battle against the inevitable? Her mind insisted on a walk about the grounds, a silent search for undefined clues.

Perhaps Rosa could be a friend, an ally, Lisa reasoned as she walked slowly about the grounds. Rosa had been here forever. She knew everybody who had ever set foot in the villa. Rosa must have known Lisa's father, her half-brother. From the very first, without her mother's putting it into words, logic had conveyed to Lisa that this missing brother had shared a father with her but was borne by a different mother.

Lisa stopped beside a fountain and allowed one hand to brush through the cool spray. Her eyes rested contemplatively on the shuttered wing of the house. The left wing was closed, Pia had said, implying that this was due to the shortage of servants.

Impulsively, Lisa strode ahead, anxious now for a better glimpse of the closed wing of the villa. Shutters on every floor were shut tight. Vines crawled high against the wall, as though joyous at the lack of attention. A heavy fragrance enticed Lisa closer. This section of the garden grew unfettered by requirements for uniformity. Its lushness captivated Lisa.

"What are you doing here?" a voice, harsh and guttural, lashed out. "You have no right!"

Lisa swerved, surprised by the unexpected voice. A man, well over six feet, with massive shoulders, stood above her on a terrace. He was dressed in chinos and a dark shirt. His gray-sprinkled hair was cropped close to his head. His face was etched with fury. German, Lisa guessed, identifying the accent.

"I'm sorry," Lisa stammered, raising her voice so that it would carry across to the man on the terrace. "I was just strolling about the grounds."

"This part is not for guests." The man was making an effort to conceal his anger, yet from the way he held his body, Lisa knew he raged inside. "Go please.

You do not come this way again!" The threat was veiled yet ominous. This was a man with whom one did not argue.

Lisa spun about and walked rapidly back along the path that had brought her there. Her heart was pounding. The man on the terrace had looked angry enough to kill.

THREE

Lisa retreated to the sequestered corner of the garden she had chosen for work. She was still shaken from her encounter with the massive, brusque German. His fury had unnerved her more than she cared to admit. She glanced tentatively towards the villa, guessing that it was time for lunch.

Lisa packed up her paints and telescoped her easel into carrying position. She headed back for the house, taking a roundabout route along the lake. Scott was sprawled comfortably in a chaise on the terrace that faced the lake. A book lay flipped open, face down, across Scott's lap, as though the view had been more potent than the printed word.

"I was just about to go searching for you," he called, with the indulgent tones accorded an affectionately regarded child. "Come sit down. Lunch will be brought in a few minutes."

Almost crossly, Lisa walked up the steps to the terrace and plopped down into a cushioned chair.

of her mind Lisa was preparing herself for some exchange about the man who had halted her walking tour of the grounds. No reason for *her* to feel guilty. Rather, for the countess and Pia to come forth with explanations.

Pia excused herself the instant luncheon could be considered finished. Scott returned to the chaise, picked up his book. Lisa hesitated, burning to confide the morning's mystery, yet feeling self-conscious about discussing it with Scott.

"Siesta time," she shrugged, heading to collect her painting equipment. "See you." For an instant her eyes met his, and a strange excitement took root. For a moment Scott and she were off on an island of their own, away from the world. Scott's eyes were admiring as they swept over her. She was still too white, Lisa thought impatiently—she would have to lie in the sun for the golden Italian look.

"Need some help with that?" Scott offered.

"I can manage, thank you," she said crisply, almost with defiance. But for once he was not looking at her as though she might be a spoiled younger sister. If they had been back home, he probably would have been on the verge of asking for a date, Lisa guessed.

"If you run into trouble, yell for help," Scott offered offhandedly.

In her room Lisa noted that the bed had been made, minor disorder straightened, the windows shut, shutters closed against the daytime heat. Lisa crossed to the windows and opened them, leaving the shutters partly closed to keep the room in shade. She stretched, yawned, and capitulated to nature. When in Rome, do as the Romans do. A nap would go well now.

Lisa awoke refreshed. Pleasant afternoon shadows filled the room. Here and there a splash of sun darted between the slats of the shutters to lay its golden warmth across the green carpets.

She could hear Scott moving about his room slowly, like a man pacing deep in thought. Scott created the air of having a leisurely approach to life, a casual attitude that, to Lisa, was suspect. There was a strength in his ruggedly good-looking face, an intensity in the hazel eyes that betrayed him.

She rose from the bed and went into the bathroom to try the vintage shower. She undressed and stepped into the large, low tub. The icy, exhilarating water chased away some of the tension that had closed in about her.

When she stepped from the shower Lisa could hear the typewriter in the next room. It was legitimate typing now, though hunt and peck. She could be completely wrong about Scott, Lisa forced herself to concede. He might be a writer specializing in the art field. He said that he had done a series on tapestries. She was probably reading hidden meanings into everything.

Lisa dressed swiftly, donning a jersy printed sheath which was now as fresh and unrumpled as when she had bought it. Pia had told her at luncheon to leave out whatever needed to be pressed for Maria to do in the morning. What a marvelously uncluttered way of living, yet Pia Menotti seemed restless, discontent, every time Lisa saw her. Much too quiet a life for Pia. But now that Scott was here, Pia might find the villa less lonely. The tall German, Lisa wondered . . . how did he fit into Pia's life? Thinking about him objectively, Lisa recognized a strong, masculine quality in the man that many women would find attractive.

Lisa straightened up, alert to a whistle that penetrated the half-closed shutters. Scott was apparently signaling. She walked to the balcony, threw open the shuttered door and leaned forward.

"I knew you were awake," Scott greeted her exuberantly. "What do you say we go for a tour of the grounds? Everybody else will be asleep for hours." He grinned persuasively.

"All right," she agreed. Maybe she could, very casually, say something about the man this morning. She was suddenly impatient for Scott's reaction. She had been disappointed that nothing was said at lunch, either in apology or censure.

"Meet me downstairs on the terrace in five minutes," Scott ordered in high good humor. "Don't keep me waiting." A glint of amusement showed in his eyes. "After all, I'm the only man about the place." For an instant his glance tangled with hers—speculative, approving. Scott had a way of looking at her that suggested he did not fully trust his own instincts, which was oddly intriguing.

Lisa closed the door again and ran to inspect herself in the mirror. Frowning at the shadowed reflection, she barely touched her mouth with fresh lipstick, brushed powder across her nose. She was not in competition with the Italian-movie-star look that Pia pursued.

Scott greeted her on the terrace. "Have you any idea how enormous these grounds are? I was talking with the contessa this morning. The property extends clear across to the edge of the lake."

"It must be worth a fortune," Lisa murmured. Again she wondered what there was here at the Villa Como that belonged to her, Lisa Kirby. The Kirby belonged to her only as a technicality. In reality, she was half-Italian, Lisa surmised. Not German? Could that hulk of a man this morning be in some way connected with her? She recoiled from the prospect, for the first time aware that finding a missing brother might be something other than pleasurable.

Her mother had not been out of the country, except for those six weeks in Mexico last summer, since the years of World War II. How old would her brother be? Older than she, most certainly! Or was this taking too much for granted? The brother could have been born after her. Was there a Menotti relative off at school somewhere? But this was summer, school was out. Yet there *could* be a younger brother, off somewhere. The child of one of the Menotti men who took refuge at the villa during the war years? But now the villa was deserted, except for the contessa and Pia. How was she to discover what her mother had so urgently commanded?

"Which direction shall we take?" Scott asked, an undertone of tension in his voice.

"Around this way," Lisa said quickly, indicating a direction away from the villa to the right, clear of the closed left wing.

"We'll have to inquire about a boat one of these

days," Scott said, scanning the lake below. "I haven't seen a sign of one on this side of the water."

Lisa was as conscious of the implication that Scott and she would be spending time together, as she was conscious of his hand at her elbow.

"I had a rather strange experience this morning," she said for a forced lightness. Her heart was pounding as she remembered.

"What happened?" Scott asked.

"I went wandering around in the gardens on the other side," she went on, her words almost stumbling over one another in her anxiety to confide. "I was sure I was within the villa property. How wrong can you be?" she laughed self-consciously. "The way the grounds are walled in for what seems like miles around!" She caught her breath for an instant, visualizing the huge figure of the furious man on the terrace above her.

"So what jumped out from behind a bush to frighten you?" he said half jokingly.

"I was walking in the direction of the left wing, the part of the villa the contessa said was closed." Lisa spoke slowly, striving for casualness. "Suddenly this man pops out on the terrace over on that side. He was livid because I was there. He ordered me back to the villa."

"What did he look like?" Scott still kept on a facade of raillery.

"Don't you believe me?" Lisa challenged, blue eyes ablaze. When was Scott Anderson going to stop playing games with her?

"I believe you," he said quietly, his hand at her

elbow prodding her down the path because she had stopped dead. He cast a cautious glance over his shoulders, as though to make sure they were not being followed. "What about the man?"

"He was very tall, about forty, with a German accent. Yes, I'm sure it was German. He bellowed at me for being there, ordered me to get out fast—"

"You say anything to Pia?"

"No. I half expected her to say something to me," Lisa admitted. "He acted as though I had behaved in some unpardonable fashion. But nobody had said that we couldn't explore anywhere about the villa!"

"Let's take ourselves a roundabout walk," Scott said softly. "To the rear of the villa and out around the left wing."

"Scott, do we dare?" Her blue eyes widened in doubt. Scott had believed her. He had not even seemed terribly surprised, just anxious for information.

"It's broad daylight. You're with me." His eyes rested on her with a humorously reproachful glint. "Scared?"

"No," she said honestly.

"Then let's walk."

They walked briskly but without suspicious haste along the paths through the rear gardens.

"Through here," Scott murmured softly. He discovered a narrow side path that would skirt within thirty feet of the sweeping terrace of the left wing.

All the windows were shuttered, Lisa noted now. She was conscious that Scott's eyes, too, were sweeping over the closed wing. Ostensibly, there were no signs of anyone living in the wing. Even the greenery had been permitted to grow into an abandoned lushness, in contrast to the well-kept grounds about the other wing of the villa.

Scott reached for Lisa's hand, held it firmly in his, all the while talking lightly about the olive groves, the lemon terraces and the Italian climate.

"Fermu!" a voice rang out with jarring harshness.

Scott's hand tightened about hers as they turned towards the dark-shirted man on the terrace. It was the same massive stranger Lisa had encountered that morning—with one change. He now wore a holster at his waist. One hand rested on the handle of a gun, waiting in readiness.

"What is it?" Scott's voice was deceptively cool. There was a flicker of contempt in his eyes as they traveled to the gun. "Are they shooting a film on the villa grounds today?"

"The signorina knows," the man barked tersely. "She was told this morning. This side of the villa is closed. No one is to travel here." The man appeared uneasy now before Scott's calm. "Please leave."

"This is still the Villa Como?" Scott inquired with excessive politeness. "I understand the property extends beyond the olive groves there."

Lisa tugged futilely at his arm. The gun was no stage prop.

"This is not an area for guests," the man repeated impatiently. "Leave!"

"Scott, please," Lisa whispered. "Let's go."

They walked quickly, in silence, towards the sector of the gardens where Lisa had worked that morning.

"What do you think?" Lisa asked somberly when they were a comfortable hundred yards clear.

"I don't know. But we'll ask some questions at dinner tonight," he promised, frowning in thought. "No sense pretending it never happened. He's sure to report our being there."

"Why should we pretend it never happened?" Lisa asked indignantly. Then she was silent. The realization that Scott was out for some answers of his own and would have preferred not to make an open issue of this was disquieting.

Lisa dressed for dinner—needing the support of being socially correct. Mascara tonight for the thickly curling lashes and an irridescent blue shadow that emphasized the near-purple of her eyes. She chose a black silk knit that was more sophisticated than anything she normally wore. She refused to admit, even to herself, that she was dressing for Scott Anderson. Or that she wanted to claim for herself some of the glances Pia's swinging, earthy torso succeeded in getting.

Lisa studied her reflection in the mirror confident that Scott would take a second look tonight. The silk knit clung to her small, high bosom, tiny waist, slim hips. Her absurdly high-heeled sandals were becoming. The locket achieved an aura of importance against the black sheen of her dress.

She listened intently, waiting for Scott to leave his room. Was it so important to make an impression on Scott, she now wondered. Yet she could not bring herself to leave her room until Scott was downstairs, knowing the entrance she could make descending the wide marble staircase.

Guiltily aware of the reasons for her late approach to dinner, Lisa walked with her head held high. Scott spied her when she was only a few steps from the bottom of the stairs.

"Cocktails tonight, American style," Scott announced, walking to meet her. His voice dropped to a whisper as he reached her side. "I haven't said anything yet about our Gestapo-type friend. Let me introduce it later, all right?" His persuasive smile was in sharp contrast to the coldness in his eyes. He was more disturbed than he had allowed her to believe, Lisa realized. "I'm not sure we ought to serve you whiskey," he teased, his voice loud enough to be heard by the others. "What's the legal age in Italy?"

"They drink wine at ten months," Lisa tossed back. "I would have been drinking martinis years ago."

The contessa was seated on the brocade sofa dressed in an ankle-length black gown, her aged neck encased in strands of pearls. Her faded eyes were heavily made up and her hair meticulously coiffed. Tonight, anyone could see that the contessa must have been a reigning beauty in her day.

"My husband," the contessa said condescendingly, "would have had no part of your American drinks. It was his opinion that good whiskey should never be disguised."

"There are many Americans," Scott chuckled, "who share that opinion."

He was charmingly deferential in his manner towards the contessa. However, the contessa seemed to be struggling against ill temper. Twice, Lisa intercepted a look of veiled anger flowing from the contessa to Pia, though the contessa was responding to Scott's determined efforts to ingratiate himself.

"You might make the grade as a bartender in some

Third Avenue gin mill," Lisa jibed, smiling at Scott. "I've had worse martinis."

"What is this Third Avenue gin mill?" Pia inquired, her heavy-lidded eyes provocatively settled on Scott. Her dress was cut daringly low. Her naturally golden skin had been darkened by the sun and contrasted strikingly with the white she seemed to favor.

"Oh, like something you run into on—" He cut short his explanation, as though alerting himself to caution. "A rather plebeian bar such as one might come across in Milan or Rome—not fashionable or populated by the neighborhood crew." His eyes were clouded and a faint smile hovered about his mouth. He's relieved at having avoided a misstep, Lisa thought. What was it Scott had almost said?

"Il pranzo e servito," Rosa called.

"I'm really going to be spoiled around here," Scott chortled, offering his arm to the contessa with mock gallantry. "Surrounded by beautiful women."

For an instant Scott's glance encountered Lisa's, both of them mindful of the fact that the villa was not as maleless as the contessa and Pia professed.

"The locket you wear, Miss Kirby," the contessa questioned. "Is it a family treasure?"

"My father brought it back from Italy when he was in service," Lisa explained, searching for meaning behind the contessa's interest.

"Your father was here during the war?" The contessa was making an effort to mask the urgency in her voice. "Here near Milan?"

Lisa settled herself gracefully in the chair Pia indicated. She sat to the contessa's left, Scott to her right. Pia sat at the opposite end of the magnificent formal dining table. Its exquisite lace tablecloth, on closer inspection, proved to be mended in many areas with delicate stitches. A chandelier, a miniature of the showpiece that hung in the foyer, lent an air of grandeur to the dinner Maria was placing before them. Asparagus soup, served in delicate gold-rimmed bowls, was the first course.

"My father fought through Africa, Sardinia and southern Italy," Lisa improvised slowly. "He was never fortunate enough to travel above Rome." Her heart pounded beneath the black knit as she reached for her spoon.

"During the war years, that might have been considered fortunate," Scott contributed. "He wasn't up in the front lines."

"But this was all before your time, my dear." The contessa made a point of being charming to Lisa. "The locket is beautiful."

Rosa waddled in to remove the soup plates and beamingly accepted the compliments of the diners. Behind her, Maria traveled with dinner plates, piled high with chicken Tetrazzini, delicate miniature carrots, fresh peas. Wine glasses were filled. Maria skipped back into the room, swinging her full hips, carrying a cut-glass salad bowl.

Involuntarily, Lisa kept glancing at Scott, waiting for him to puncture the serenity of the table with inquiries about the stranger.

"I expect to sleep like the dead tonight," Scott announced, digging with enthusiasm into the chicken. "Americans away from home have a habit of overeating and overwalking. Lisa and I both cut short our siestas this afternoon. We joined forces for a tour of the grounds."

There was a set smile about the contessa's face, a steely coldness in her eyes as she listened with forced politeness. "Oh yes, I gather you spoke with the man at the left wing," she said calmly.

"That's a delicate way of phrasing it," Scott grinned. "He practically pointed a gun at our heads."

"Really, Pia," the contessa said with a display of annoyance, "you must speak to Signor Obermann about his uncouth approach to people." Her eyes moved to Pia for just an instant, but Lisa caught the hostility between the two women and the inference that Signor Obermann was Pia Menotti's responsibility.

"We had no intention of trespassing," Scott continued smoothly. "There was nothing said about any part of the grounds being out of bounds." He was forcing the explanation upon them.

"The left wing is structurally unsound," Pia said stiffly, dark eyes smoldering. "Signor Obermann is an engineer, here to make a study of the necessary repairs. I am sorry that he was brusque."

The conversation turned to other matters, but Lisa's mind continued to dwell on the brief exchange about Obermann. He was the man for whom the smoking tobacco was probably intended, she decided in disappointment. It was going to be a rough assignment to discover a link to her brother here at the villa. Perhaps her mother had been overly optimistic, forgetful of the passage of time. The locket held no significance for the contessa or for

Rosa, the only two members of the Menotti household who belonged to the era when her mother was here. For whom would it hold meaning? Certainly not the three English school teachers traipsing around the countryside? For the first time, misgivings about her chasing off to Italy stirred within Lisa.

Lisa went tiredly about the routine of preparing for sleep. The heat of the afternoon, the tension of dinner, the doubts preying upon her, had taken away her normal ebullience. A cool wind from the mountains was peacefully refreshing.

Lisa walked to the balcony, opened the shuttered door to gaze out upon the lake shimmering beneath the near-full moon. She gazed at the dark shadows of twin mountains in the distance that met like a pair of voluptuous breasts. She could understand her mother's obsession for the beauty of Italy.

Why had her mother never returned, Lisa asked herself. Why was the summer in the Italy they had promised themselves always "next year"? For her mother there would never be a next year. Her throat tightened as she remembered. She owed it to her mother to carry out that last exhortation. "Find your brother—find what belongs to you." Tears stung her eyelids, loneliness closed in on her. The cool wind from the mountains turned cold. The moon hid behind clouds and the serenity of the night disappeared.

Lisa started at the sound of a light knock on her door.

"Entree," she called softly, half-expecting her visitor to be Scott.

The door opened, and Rosa waddled in, a blanket cradled in her fat arms.

"Tonight the *vento*," Rosa said, gesturing towards the open door to the balcony. "This will be good." She walked to the bed with the blanket and placed it across the foot.

"Thank you, Rosa." Lisa smiled, fighting an impulse to talk to Rosa about her mother in the hopes that she might remember her.

"Close," Rosa said firmly. "Tonight *freddo*." Rosa hugged her arms to back up her lack of English. She seemed reluctant to leave the room. Uneasy.

Was it the prospect of a cold mountain wind—or some less innocuous intruder—that caused the trepidation in Rosa's eyes? A chill settled about Lisa. Why was Rosa locking the shutters? Lisa reminded herself sharply that she couldn't afford to cater to girlish fears. Now was the moment to probe.

"You've been with the contessa for many years, haven't you, Rosa?" Lisa's voice was warm, friendly. "You must have known the contessa's son, the signora's husband?"

Rosa's face paled. "I knew." She seemed to be involved in an inner battle.

"When did he die?" Lisa asked, suddenly trembling inside. "It must have been tragic, for a man so young."

"Signorina Kirby," Rosa pleaded in a husky whisper, "leave the Villa Como! Leave!"

As Lisa stared in open-mouthed astonishment, Rosa whirled about and hurried from the room at a speed Lisa would have thought impossible, considering her weight. Rosa's brief impassioned warning had been laden with honest concern for Lisa.

Lisa walked back to the balcony, pushed open the shuttered door and stared out into the night. Clouds gathered overhead into great clumps of blackness; the wind howled down from the mountains. Rosa's ominous words echoed in her mind. But she couldn't leave now, Lisa reminded herself, fighting against panic. Not without answers!

FOUR

The *vento* of the night before had become a gentle breeze. Lisa sat on the balcony before her breakfast tray thinking over all that had happened since her arrival. She knew that Scott had been restless far into the night, despite his prediction that he would sleep like the dead.

The morning sun was high. She had slept far later than she had planned and felt guilty because the time might have been spent in more rewarding pursuit.

There was a light tap at her door.

"Lisa?" Scott whispered from the hall.

"Come in," she called back.

Scott opened the door and strolled nonchalantly across the room to the balcony, making a point of leaving the door wide open. "I was beginning to wonder if you were going to sleep all day, but Maria said you were breakfasting. I've rented a car for the day.

It'll be brought up any time now. Let's treat ourselves to a day of roaming around the countryside," he coaxed.

"I should be working," Lisa hedged.

"You'll work tomorrow," Scott decreed. "Meet me downstairs in ten minutes. I'll tell Pia we won't be at the villa for lunch."

"Scott," Lisa halted him.

"Yes?"

Lisa walked swiftly to the door, closed it. "Scott, do you believe that business about the left wing being structurally unsound? Do you think Obermann is here for that reason?"

"Have I any reason to doubt it?" Scott lifted an eyebrow, in a show of amusement. "Maybe Obermann is Pia's lover, and the contessa disapproves." He brushed Lisa's chin in a gesture of affection. "See you in ten minutes. And stop making big productions out of little incidents."

Scott, too, had noticed the contessa's disapproval of Obermann. Why did the contessa allow him to be about the villa? Who else was here that the guests knew nothing about? Her brother? If only she dared to confide in Scott, to enlist his help.

When Lisa came downstairs, Scott was on the terrace drinking coffee with Pia. They talked in low tones which kept the subject matter of their conversation a secret. In the driveway below, a green Fiat waited.

"Good morning," Scott greeted her briskly, pushing back his chair.

"Good morning, Miss Kirby," Pia said in her precise English.

"Are we ready to shove off?" Lisa asked, feeling festive and carefree. Pia Menotti was probably wondering why Scott bothered to tag after a snip of an American girl. Well, he did bother, she reminded herself in triumph, and she was exhilarated by the prospect of a day alone with Scott Anderson.

With Scott's hand at her elbow, they walked jauntily down the stairs to the car. Lisa was conscious that Pia's gaze followed them.

"There's a little town six miles to the west along the lake," Scott said as he seated himself behind the wheel. "I hear it's just bristling with local color. Maybe you should have brought along a sketch pad."

"Not today."

"We'll take care of some errands at the same time," Scott continued casually. "We'll stop off at the *tintoria*—the dry-cleaning store," Scott interpreted, and Lisa caught herself on the verge of saying "I know." Scott reached into his pocket for cigarettes, extracted one, extended the pack to Lisa, who shook her head. His hand shot back to the wheel as a trio of Vespas zoomed past, and he swore under his breath. "Scrounge around in my jacket for matches, will you, honey?"

"One moment." An unfamiliar warmth prickled her skin as she searched in his jacket pocket for a pad of matches. Ought she to confide in Scott? She felt so completely at sea in the strange surroundings, and inadequate to the assignment ahead. "Here they are." She extracted a match and, striking it, held it so that Scott could light his cigarette. She was very conscious of his rugged strength and his warmth.

"I have a pile of slacks and shirts to be done. One

valise was loaded with soiled clothes. I should have asked you if you had anything to—"

"I have nothing for the *tintoria*," she said, deliberately slurring the word. Her quick mind clutched at this new tidbit. If Scott had arrived—as he *said*—from five weeks in London, why had he showed up at the villa with a valise full of soiled clothes? Instinct told Lisa that Scott Anderson was too meticulous an individual not to take his clothes to the cleaners before such a trip. She guessed that Scott had come to the Villa Como on a hastily reached decision, leaving no time for the amenities. She could not resist the impulse to probe. "You were lucky to get accommodations at the villa on such short notice."

"Did I say it was short notice?" he asked guardedly.

"Pia Menotti mentioned something about it," Lisa lied, watching to see if Scott would buy it. "I wrote two months ahead, and this was the first vacancy available."

"How did you happen to settle on the Villa Como?" Scott asked, his eyes on the curving road ahead.

"I liked the idea of only a handful of guests. And I really decided on impulse," Lisa fabricated breathlessly. "What about you?"

"I closed my eyes and pointed," he chuckled. "You can never tell anything from the brochures."

They were both lying, of course, Lisa acknowledged, sliding back into a somber mood. How could she confide in Scott until she knew more about him and his reasons for being there? Lisa sighed. She was young and in Italy and out for a day's sightseeing with a good-looking man. It should be marvelous fun

—except that she was haunted by her real mission.

"Maria gave me a tip about a restaurant for lunch," Scott said. "It's owned by a cousin of her mother's. We're to get preferential treatment."

"Sounds great," Lisa said, trying to regain her air of conviviality. She sensed that Scott, too, was making a determined effort to be casual. But he had a way of narrowing his eyes and staring off into space that hinted of anxiety.

"You didn't sleep last night," he said with a note of concern when she struggled to stifle a yawn. "I heard you prowling around till all hours."

"Is that what you do for amusement?" she shot back defensively. "Keep track of everyone's personal habits?"

"I'm used to sleeping till noon, carousing till daybreak," he apologized. "Tough to break that habit. Besides," he grinned, "I have a writer's curiosity about people."

They sped in companionable silence along the lake road. Scott broke the silence now and then to point out something of minor interest. Suddenly Lisa realized that Scott Anderson must have been at the villa —or near it—before this trip.

"Imagine doing the family laundry like that?" Scott chuckled, nodding towards a cluster of women at one side of the lake. They were dipping clothes, swatting them against old-fashioned washboards. The sound of their voices in good-humored conversation made an unintelligible murmur.

"Not quite like suburbia," Lisa conceded.

"I can't imagine you in suburbia," Scott said. The way he said it was a compliment. "City girl, right?"

"New York," she said, gazing ahead. At this moment she preferred not to think about New York.

"My town, too, except for periods of escape. But it's a nice feeling to know it's always there."

For an instant his eyes met hers, saying much.

"There's the village," she said, feeling slightly uncomfortable because she was wondering what it would be like to be kissed by Scott Anderson.

The village spread before them, a cluster of stuccoed houses encircling an astonishingly elegant church. There was a row of shops and a Piazza where mothers sat in the hot sun while children played and old people rested and gossiped.

"There's the restaurant," Scott said briskly.

Lisa turned from an inspection of the shops to look at the low building he had indicated. A handful of tables set out in front were empty except for a pair of middleaged Americans nibbling at ices.

"It's early for lunch," Lisa warned.

"Not for tourists," he reminded her. "Let's eat inside. It'll be cooler under the fans."

All through the leisurely luncheon, which Scott ordered with charming adherence to the waitress' suggestions, Lisa sensed that he was waiting for something. The restlessness that he had barely managed to conceal came out into the open. The trip had not been on impulse, after all. It had been planned, with an objective in mind; but whatever it might be, it had failed to materialize. Lisa was relieved that she had remained reticent with Scott.

After they left the restaurant, Scott seemed to relax again and made a point of amusing Lisa with light banter. Back in New York, Lisa thought wistfully, she would be soaring on the clouds if Scott Anderson had come along and made a play for her. When they happened to touch accidentally, now and then through the afternoon, Lisa was aware of the electric charge that shot through her and suspected an echo in Scott.

She felt an odd regret when they were in the car again en route to the villa. It had been an unexpectedly relaxing day, which at this point she needed. She sat back in a serene silence during the return trip. She exchanged a smile of mutual satisfaction with Scott as he slowed down at the approach to the gate.

"It was fun," Lisa said softly as the villa gate closed behind them.

"I thought so, too," Scott concurred, a hand dropping across one of Lisa's. He leaned forward; his mouth grazed hers. "You're a sweet one, Lisa Kirby."

Lisa sat back against the door on her side of the car. She had wanted Scott Anderson to kiss her! But she felt cheated because it had been such a swift, fragmentary thing. And already she sensed that Scott was retreating. The condescension in his voice had hurt her. "A sweet one," indeed!

As they drove up to the villa, a taxi was pulled away, leaving a pile of luggage on the terrace. Lisa surmised that the other guests had returned to the villa.

The house was still with the quietness of siesta time. Now and then Lisa heard feminine voices that she guessed belonged to the three Englishwomen, who appeared to be settling themselves in two rooms at the extreme end of the corridor. She would make friends with them, Lisa promised herself firmly, because they might afford her some clues.

The contessa had said there would be a tea laid on the terrace in late afternoons, Lisa recalled. Probably out of deference for the English guests. Today Lisa herself was in a tea mood. There was something strangely reassuring about sipping tea and nibbling small sandwiches in surroundings such as these.

She walked quietly from her room and headed for the stairs, enjoying the solitude of the villa. She paused for a moment before the fake Modigliani. Tonight, she would just relax, forget about everything, Lisa promised herself. Tomorrow, with a good night's sleep behind her, she would be able to think more clearly, to map out a strategy.

She walked through the doorway that led to the west terrace. Too early for tea, obviously. There was no sign of a table laid, or even of Maria or Rosa making preparations. She still had to learn to relax into the Italian tempo, Lisa admonished herself. She sat down at the edge of a chaise, uncertain as to how to spend these leisurely moments.

Laughter from down below drew her attention. She leaned over the railing to see whose it was. Pia, with Scott, as she had supposed. They were walking down a narrow path that led to the beach. Pia was in a black and white polka-dot bikini with a cerise towel casually draped across one arm. Scott wore plaid swimming trunks. Lisa's pulse quickened. She felt sick as she watched Pia slide an arm through Scott's and sway towards him in the intimate manner of a woman attracted to a man and determined to let him know.

Lisa spied another path that would lead down to the beach, probably winding up a comfortable distance from the strip of beach where Scott and Pia would arrive. She whirled away from the railing and headed into the house again. Jealousy was an unfamiliar emotion for Lisa Kirby to feel and it shamed her even as it pained her.

She rushed up the stairs to her room, glad that she had brought two new swim suits. Her hands were unsteady as she pulled a turquoise suit from a hanger in the closet and hurried to change. She was no Pia Menotti, Lisa decided regretfully as she inspected her reflection in the mirror. There was none of the overwhelming earthiness of Pia's figure about her slim body. She had small high breasts, an incredibly slim waist, narrow hips, long, supple thighs and legs. She had once taken pride in that figure.

Pia Menotti looked like a woman, Lisa decided unhappily, while she was built like one of a thousand girls who poured themselves into swimsuits every summer and walked off with some small-town beauty trophy. Why should a man like Scott Anderson bother about Lisa Kirby when Pia Menotti was obviously panting to make herself available?

Nevertheless, Lisa took time out to retouch her lipstick and to add a bit of eyeshadow before she headed outdoors again. Walking swiftly through the gardens, a towel slung over her arm, she deliberately took the path away from the other two. But she caught herself listening for the sound of their voices.

She emerged from the thick foliage onto the white sandy beach and for a moment was completely enthralled by the beauty of the glistening blue water beneath the afternoon sun. Far across the lake, two sailboats skimmed along the water. The perfect Italian postcard view, Lisa thought, filled with the loveliness of everything that met her gaze. Then her eyes swept down the beach and she saw Pia and Scott in good-humored argument about how to launch a small sailboat.

"Hi!" Scott called with surprise.

"Hi!" Lisa called back, wishing now that she had not made this trek down to the beach. Would Scott think she had followed him down here? Was he so confident that Pia and he would have the beach to themselves during the siesta hours?

Deliberately, Lisa dropped her towel on the white sand and hurried out into the lake, welcoming the afternoon warmth of the water. She took care to swim close to shore because she knew in a few minutes she would head back to the house. Would Scott think she had trailed them out here? she wondered. She was miserable and full of self-reproach. Is that how it would look to Pia, too? Her face felt hot as she listened to their laughter.

For a moment, as Lisa walked towards the path that would take her back to the house, she thought she heard Scott yelling her name. She refused to slow down. She had no wish to stand beside Pia, she decided in childlike belligerence, so that Scott Anderson could compare her with his overblown Italian. Why did American men make such a fetish of bosoms? Not that she was lacking, Lisa told herself. It was just that Pia was so abundantly endowed.

Lisa stopped for a few moments on the terrace to make sure she had dried herself well. When only the ends of her hair were slightly damp, she decided that she could walk into the house without causing damage. Nevertheless, because her sandals bore vestiges of sand, she slid them from her feet and carried them in one hand.

She was about to go up the stairs when the sound of a door swinging in the breeze caught her attention. Lisa followed the sound through a large room and then a smaller one, both unfamiliar to her. She discovered that the banging was caused by an ornate oak door on a small room that at first appeared to be a closet.

She peered with mounting curiosity into the tiny room. It was lined on three sides with bookshelves. On the fourth wall was an oil painting of a young boy of about eight or nine. A modern painting done by someone with talent, Lisa judged with respect. Something about the subject was oddly disturbing to her.

Lisa walked into the room and stood before the portrait. An excellent artist, she decided, startled by the tremor of excitement than ran through her. Who was the artist? Who was the subject? Lisa had an eerie sensation of looking at someone she knew from another era of her life.

"What are you doing in this part of the house, Miss Kirby?" the contessa's voice, icy with rage, rang through the silence.

Lisa whirled about. She was embarrassed to be

found standing there, barefoot and in a wet bathing suit amidst such elegance. "I'm sorry," she faltered, color flooding her face.

"This is the family part of the house," the contessa continued. She sought to control her anger. "I do not open these rooms to guests."

"The door was banging," Lisa tried to explain. "I walked in here without thinking—" The question was plaguing her now: Who *was* the boy in the portrait?

The contessa relaxed the sharpness of her voice. "Please remember in the future. I am sure there are ample facilities for your comfort."

"It's a beautiful painting," Lisa said on impulse, eyeing the contessa. "A member of the family?"

"My stepson, many years ago," the contessa said, almost indifferently. "Now if you will please excuse me."

"Of course," Lisa said with an ironic politeness that echoed the contessa's.

Lisa walked swiftly from the tiny room to the part of the house with which she was familiar. For an instant she stopped dead, startled. Scott was standing there; he had been eavesdropping on the brief exchange. Before she could open her mouth to say anything Scott managed to disappear.

Lisa frowned as she continued her way to the staircase. Why had Scott been eavesdropping? Why had he made a point of disappearing at her approach? What was there about the portrait of the blue-eyed, dark-haired boy whom the contessa identified as a stepson, that tugged at some cavern of her own memory? What was she to believe, *whom* was she to believe, within the walls of the Villa Como?

FIVE

Lisa hung her wet bathing suit across the antiquated shower ring above the tub. Slowly she dressed again in a casual lemon-yellow shift that would acquire a more formal note with pearls. No, not pearls, Lisa remembered, reaching instead for the locket. Somewhere in this village, there was a man—or a woman—for whom her mother's treasured locket would hold meaning.

Perhaps she was wrong in centering her search solely within the villa, Lisa thought somberly. She could be narrowing her horizon too finely. The village itself had been almost a part of the villa many years ago. She would make a point of spending some time in the small shops and the restaurants, Lisa decided with a fresh surge of determination.

From the corridor, she heard the high-pitched voices of the three Englishwomen in good-humored debate over the highlights of their trip to Venice. They were descending the staircase now, intent on their afternoon tea. Lisa was suddenly reluctant to join the other guests on the terrace. She was in no mood for new faces. She walked across to the balcony and opened the shuttered doors. She heard Maria singing somewhere downstairs, then an annoyed command from the contessa.

What had been so terrible about her walking back into the house that way? Lisa asked herself defensively. What was there about the simple act of her walking through impersonal rooms to stop a door from banging that merited the contessa's fury? The contessa said the portrait was that of her stepson. Was the stepson Pia's husband? Was the stepson the child of a second husband?

In the next room the uneven pecking at a typewriter began. Scott was making a stab at convincing the English ladies that he was, in reality, a writer. Was she being childish in not believing him? Lisa asked herself uneasily. She stiffened to attention as her eye caught a movement far below in the gardens. Leaning forward intently, she identified the figure of the man the contessa had called Signor Obermann.

She watched with fascination. Someone was walking toward him now. A woman in a short, white hooded beach jacket. Obermann and the woman came together in passionate embrace. The hood fell away as the woman's mouth clung to Obermann's. Pia Menotti.

"Interesting," a male voice drawled softly. Lisa swung about to discover Scott on his own balcony, sharing her view. "Why aren't you downstairs having tea with the three school teachers?" he chided.

"I wasn't interested in tea," Lisa replied. If Scott were interested in Pia, the view below would do much to dispel that interest. She felt better.

"I still have the car," Scott informed her. "What about our doing some night-crawling around town?"

"Tonight?" Lisa lifted an eyebrow in surprise.

"Why not? The car won't be picked up until tomorrow. The agency phoned. We might as well live dangerously. Dinner, some carousing about the local night life."

"Might be fun," Lisa conceded. "When?"

"Suppose we leave about eight?" he offered. "We'll be early enough to miss the dinner crowds. Believe it or not," he grinned, "these hills abound in tourists."

"Eight o'clock," Lisa agreed. "Do I need to dress?" she asked uncertainly.

"You're fine like that," he approved, his eyes trailing over the lemon-yellow sheath. "I'll get down to work, so I won't feel guilty about gadding about again." He returned to his room and began clicking away on the typewriter.

Scott made such a point of stressing his profession, Lisa thought. But she was sure that it was some kind of cover. Anyhow, he was taking her out tonight, she reminded herself. To get back at Pia? She would hate that, being a pawn in some affair between Scott and Pia Menotti.

Lisa stretched out along the length of the bed, carefully smoothing the yellow sheath beneath her and picked up a paperback. She was secretly relieved that Scott had suggested dinner away from the villa.

Scott hadn't appeared to be at all ruffled by Pia's impassioned encounter with Obermann. The knowledge lifted her spirits, blending pleasurably with the memory of the fleeting brush of his mouth against hers. Again she dallied with the prospect of confiding in Scott. Perhaps tonight at dinner, Lisa thought. It was frightening to be alone among strangers with so much intrigue about. She recalled Rosa's warning to leave the villa. While Rosa had said nothing since, an occasional meeting of their eyes—when Rosa served a dish at the table or went about some household task in Lisa's room—told Lisa that Rosa was deeply concerned about her presence at the villa. Why?

At a few minutes before eight, Scott tapped on the door. Lisa reached for her purse and a yellow mohair stole. Then she joined him in the hall.

"Let's go," Scott greeted her briskly. "I told the contessa we wouldn't be home for dinner."

"She probably thinks we're out of our minds," Lisa giggled. The contessa was probably forming ideas of her own about why Scott and she were disappearing from the villa twice in one day. The contessa had such a supercilious attitude toward Americans. Was she slightly less haughty toward the English? Lisa wondered in amusement.

Hand in hand, caught in a mood of pleasant conspiracy, Lisa and Scott strolled down the elegant staircase.

"I quizzed Maria about another place for dinner. She's overflowing with relatives in the restaurant business," he grinned. "This place, Maria swears, has the greatest chicken Tetrazzini in all of Italy. Strike your fancy?"

"I'm starving," Lisa said pertly. "Food strikes my fancy."

The car was waiting for them in the driveway. Scott opened the door for her and waited for her to get settled, then crossed around to the other side to slide behind the wheel. Again Lisa heard the high-pitched voices of the English guests drifting down from the west terrace. She looked about in that direction and as the car shot forward her glance caught something in the foliage.

She gasped. Behind a bush, secure in the belief that he was hidden from view, Signor Obermann was watching them. Uneasiness caught hold of her as she followed Obermann's movements in the rearview mirror. He had emerged from the clump of foliage and was making his way towards the front of the house.

"Obermann's on the loose again," Lisa said with a show of casualness, but her heart was pounding.

"Heavy date with Pia?" Scott suggested, his eyes on the winding strip of road ahead of them.

"Why does he slink around that way if it's a date?" Lisa countered. "I get the impression he would rather not be observed."

"The contessa disapproves, remember?" Scott said after a moment. "Maybe he's anxious to avoid unpleasantness."

"Maybe." Lisa leaned back in her seat, looking out the window of the car but seeing nothing. If that was the way Scott wanted it to be okay; yet she sensed he was as dubious about that explanation as she was.

"This is a beautiful time of day, isn't it, Lisa?" Scott said.

"Perfect," Lisa agreed. The heat was giving way to evening coolness so that in a few moments the mohair stole would be needed.

They kept the conversation impersonal and light. Lisa suspected that only part of Scott's mind was with her. He seemed glad when they arrived in town. He parked the car, and they got to search for Maria's newest relative in the restaurant business.

They found the restaurant situated next door to the tourist hotel. The place was large and shadowy. Here and there ceiling fans provided a breeze, though the day's heat had relented.

A waiter bustled forward to greet them in a garbled mixture of English, French and Italian that brought forth smiles from both Scott and Lisa. Another waiter was hastily providing more illumination while the first led them to a table.

Lisa dropped the stole over the back of her chair while the waiter and Scott conferred over the menu. There was a comfortable family air about the restaurant that pleased her. The much-bejeweled, rotund woman behind the cash register was no doubt "Mama" and the waiters apparently were brothers or cousins. "Papa," she improvised, probably served as chef.

Behind her the second waiter switched on a wall lamp. Lisa intercepted a look of surprise on their waiter's face. His eyes were glued to the locket that rested against her yellow sheath. Lisa noted that Scott, too, was conscious of the waiter's scrutiny. What was there about her mother's locket that had shaken up the waiter?

Scott waited until the waiter had disappeared behind the swinging door that led to the kitchen.

"That locket you wear all the time," Scott began. "Valuable? I know nothing about jewelry, of course."

"Not really," Lisa said. "Sentimental trinket. My

father brought it back from Italy after the war."
Scott knew that, Lisa recalled. He had been there
when the contessa asked her about the locket. Or
would a man remember such a conversation?

"What about the stones?" Scott pursued, squinting
thoughtfully.

"Glass," Lisa said frankly, her eyes fastened to
Scott. "My mother had them appraised years ago."
It was Lisa who had taken the locket to a jeweler
days before boarding the jet that brought her
to Italy. But Scott had noticed how the waiter stared
at the locket and was searching for an explanation.
This would be a time for confidence, Lisa thought.
But the waiter returned with a bottle of wine and
glasses, and the moment was lost.

"Excuse me a moment, Lisa?" Scott said, pushing
back his chair, his glance aimed towards the counter
in the front. "I want to go over and pick up a pack of
cigarettes. I'm fresh out. I'm afraid my quota of
American cigarettes is shot."

It was difficult for Lisa to watch Scott from where
she sat. She burrowed into the interior of her small
purse for a mirror and pretended to be adjusting her
hair. Scott was in earnest conversation with the fat,
smiling woman behind the counter. Lisa saw him
head back in the direction of their table. She watched
him reach into his jacket pocket, pull out a crum-
pled pack of American cigarettes and stealthily drop
them into an ornamental urn. His last pack of American cigarettes if she could believe him.

How many times would she hover on the brink
of stupidity, Lisa upbraided herself. How could she

confide in Scott, who played games like this with her? Trust nobody, she warned herself. Not even Scott Anderson!

The waiter was placing chilled honeydew melon, served with paper thin slices of prosciutto, before them.

"How does that look?" Scott asked, beaming. "Delicious?"

"Sweet," Lisa approved, digging into the crescent of melon.

"Chicken Tetrazzini coming up," Scott grinned in anticipation. "With artichoke salad. For dessert *Fragole al Vino*—strawberries in wine—and *caffe espresso*. Disappointed?" He lifted an eyebrow in persuasive good humor.

"I'll end up fat as 'Mama' over there," Lisa whispered, "if I have dinner here very often!"

"I'll put you on bread and water," he warned. "You stay just the way you are." His eyes rested reflectively on her.

Lisa stirred beneath the intensity of his gaze. "Nothing ever stays the same, does it?" she questioned wryly.

"Profound for one so young," he teased.

"You keep talking as though I were about fourteen."

"What are you doing here, Lisa?" he questioned quietly, his eyes holding hers.

"Eating dinner," she flipped, pretending not to understand.

"What are you doing at the Villa Como?" he insisted.

"I told you," she said after a moment, color staining her cheeks. She found it impossible to confide in him now after he had made up that excuse about needing cigarettes in order to cross-examine "Mama." "I decided to live dangerously, squander a whole summer on painting in glorious Italy. I've been working at a drafting board for two years," she said with candor. "I figured it was time I found out how good I could really be at painting."

"Okay," Scott sighed. "So you're here to paint the lake. But for God's sake, Lisa, be careful." He frowned in thought. "Make sure you keep away from that creep Obermann."

As the Fiat slowed down at the villa gate, Lisa leaned towards the dashboard to look at her watch. The heavy downpour they had encountered when they left the restaurant, had subsided now. Only a fine spray of rain showed up before the headlights. It was only twenty past ten. Little of this day had been spent at the Villa Como, Lisa realized guiltily, yet the day had not been misspent.

Somehow, Lisa reflected somberly, she must get back to the restaurant, alone. Perhaps the waiter would approach her if she showed up without Scott. With luck on her side, he might provide some clue as to the true meaning of the locket. The locket *had* to be a key; her mother would not have been so insistent if it were not.

Scott parked before the impressive wrought-iron gates and left the car to phone the villa. In a few moments he was back behind the wheel.

"Someone is coming down to let us in," he reported, chuckling as he inspected her face in the shadows. "All this business with the locked gates stir your imagination?"

"I'd probably sleep with a gun under my pillow," she replied. "If I had a gun." Instantly, she was sorry she had brought up this reminder of Carl Obermann. The anxious speculation in Scott's eyes made her uneasy.

Someone was walking down the road behind the gates to admit them. They could hear the faint sound of a woman humming. Lisa's mind traveled back to the night Scott and she had arrived. The gates had been closed, but not locked. Pia had got out of the car to open the gates herself without help from the villa. Why was it so important now that the gates be locked?

In the spill of the headlights they saw Maria, walking rapidly, a kerchief over her head because the rain had not entirely subsided. Maria tugged for a few moments, then the gates swung open. Scott pulled to a stop inside the gates and opened a rear door so that Maria could scramble inside.

"*Grazie,*" Maria giggled, her eyes boldly meeting Scott's. A faint envy stole over Lisa that Maria—like Pia Menotti—could be so blatant about her interest.

When the car stopped, Maria scampered out, throwing a provocative glance at Scott. Lisa and Scott followed slowly behind her. In the drawing room, Lisa spied the cluster of women. She heard the faint clatter of china as the ladies sipped their after-dinner coffee. With an exchange of amused looks, Lisa and Scott swiftly but noiselessly slipped past the doorway to the stairs. They hurried, sharing determination not to be drawn into the evening activities.

"Thanks for dinner," Lisa said breathlessly as they reached her door.

"Be careful, you little idiot," Scott said softly.

"Of what?" Lisa challenged.

"Of gremlins," he murmured.

He took her face between his hands, and her mouth welcomed the warmth of his. Then, too soon, it was over; and she was alone before her door.

"Sleep well," she said softly, doubting that she would.

It was still early as Lisa prepared for the night. She had looked forward to lying in bed with a book, but she couldn't concentrate on the printed page.

Lisa heard the three English women, in animated conversation with Pia, walking towards their own rooms. Ten minutes later the contessa called softly from the head of the stairs, and Lisa heard Pia's cautious *"uno momento."*

The rain had stopped completely but the night winds whistled down from the mountains. A shutter swung loose and began to slam against the side of the villa with relentless rhythm. Why didn't someone go out and fix the shutter? Lisa asked herself. Putting down her book, she settled back against the large down-stuffed pillows. Would she ever fall asleep tonight?

Lisa leaned forward to switch off the lamp on the night table. Determinedly, she closed her eyes, turned on her side, and pulled the covers high above her shoulders. Sleep!

A faint relief welled in her as someone outside was grappling with the recalcitrant shutter. But the wind continued to howl through the cypress. Again Lisa thought of stormy nights in New York when she was a child; when she could scurry to the refuge of her mother's bed. She was not going to listen to the wind; she was not going to lie awake until dawn, conjuring up imaginary intruders.

Lisa was tired, and at last she slept. When she awoke, reluctantly, she knew instinctively that it was still night. And suddenly, she was fully awake, her heart pounding, her eyes staring into the darkness. Was it her imagination—or *was* there someone in this room besides herself?

Lisa lay motionless listening for sounds. The wind screeched through the trees outside. Was that *all* it was, an echo of the wind here in her room? Or was someone breathing heavily not far from her bed? Silence now. She had probably allowed her imagination to run away again, Lisa reproached herself. As a child she had been a restless sleeper, fearful of the dark, ever suspicious of intruders in the night. She would have to take hold of herself, Lisa thought grimly, while she lived here in the villa surrounded by mountain winds.

But when she tried to return to sleep, she heard a scraping noise in the dressing room as though a drawer were being opened. Lisa clutched at the bedclothes, terrified. What should she do? Rosa's warning went through her mind as did Scott's exhortations to be careful. How could you be careful with a prowler in your room?

Perhaps if she lay quiet, feigned sleep, he would find whatever he was after and leave. He, Lisa wondered, or *she?* In the dressing room, the intruder was careless; a bottle went crashing to the floor. Lisa sat upright in bed and screamed in complete terror. Her scream rose to an agonized pitch as a male figure in a raincoat dashed across the bedroom to the balcony and disappeared into the night.

"Lisa!" The door rattled as Scott called to her. "Lisa, open up!"

Trembling so that she could hardly pick up her robe, Lisa managed to make her way to the door.

"Lisa?" Scott's voice again, deep with anxiety.

"I'm coming," Lisa faltered, reaching for the door, fumbling with the key.

She swung the door open, aware of the sea of concerned faces in the corridor, then only aware that Scott was there and she was *safe*.

"Honey, what happened?" Scott pulled her close, his arms reassuringly about her shoulders.

"A man in my room," Lisa shuddered. "I thought I heard someone in the dressing room. Then a bottle crashed to the floor—"

"It's these terrible winds," the contessa said firmly. "They can be most frightening, my dear." The contessa was making an effort to be convincing. "I should have warned you."

"No," Lisa said insistently, her head burrowed against Scott's shoulder. "It was a man! I saw him race across the room towards the balcony. A tall man—" she broke off, trembling in remembrance.

"A nightmare, Miss Kirby," Pia soothed. "As the contessa said, these dreadful winds can break into your sleep when you're unfamiliar with them." Pia's gaze swept to the three Englishwomen. "Ladies, please do not be concerned."

Lisa was aware of the anxiety on the three middle-aged English faces that hovered about her.

"Let us all return to our rooms and sleep." Pia smiled with perfunctory friendliness.

Unnerved as she was, Lisa caught an angry communication between the contessa and Pia. Did the contessa suspect the intruder to be Signor Obermann? Was that the reason for the glint of cold anger in the fading blue eyes? Lisa caught herself on the verge of denying that the man could have been Obermann; he was far too slight, even in the camouflage of a belted raincoat.

But she had not imagined the tall, dark man in the belted raincoat, Lisa told herself. It had not been part of a terrible dream! The man had looked like the waiter in the restaurant tonight, Lisa realized suddenly, a coldness settling about her.

"Ladies, there has been no intruder," the contessa was saying with an air of condescension that infuriated Lisa. "The lake country in the mountains is noted for its winds. We who live here know this. We will all return to our rooms." This time it was a command.

"With your permission, Contessa," Scott said with persuasive charm, "I'll invade your kitchen and brew some coffee for Miss Kirby and myself."

"But of course," the contessa said, smiling slightly though obviously annoyed. "I trust we will all sleep well for the remainder of the night."

"I'll make sure the windows and the balcony are locked," Scott said, his hands tightening gently at Lisa's shoulders for a moment. His eyes, when they met hers, were compassionate and reassuring. "Just to make you feel better, Lisa," he added casually, aware that Pia's face had tightened in reproof.

Scott strode into the bedroom while Lisa waited uneasily by the doorway. The English ladies smiled in sympathy and moved doubtfully down the corridor towards their own rooms. If Signor Obermann were able to establish an alibi for himself, Lisa guessed, they would all be sure Lisa had imagined the whole incident.

Scott emerged from the ` dressing room and switched on every lamp in the bedroom. He carefully checked all the windows to reassure her. He was at the balcony now, checking it again. Thank heavens for Scott!

Lisa's glance trailed about the room. And then she stiffened, her eyes fastened to the carpeting. There was a trail, slight but definite, from the dressing room to the balcony. It had not been a nightmare! The shoes of her intruder had been caked with mud from the garden below.

SIX

Lisa sat hunched over a table in the corner of the huge kitchen while Scott poured coffee for them.

"My brew is wicked," he warned with a chuckle. "I get carried away in the presence of a tin of coffee."

"Scott, you don't believe I was having a nightmare, do you?" Her eyes searched his; she needed his acceptance.

"It could happen to anybody," he said carefully, stirring sugar into his coffee. "Don't feel lousy about that."

"But I didn't have a nightmare! That man was in my room. I have proof." She lifted her head high in challenge.

"What proof?" Scott asked quickly.

"Footprints on the carpeting. Mud prints. Let the contessa alibi *that* away."

"Sure they're mud prints?" Scott questioned. "Perhaps dirt stains that you hadn't noticed before?"

"Mud," Lisa insisted. "Come back upstairs with me and I'll show you." What was the matter with Scott? Why did he pretend to doubt her, she wondered impatiently.

"After we've had our coffee," he said. "Whom do you suspect?"

"I don't know." She hesitated. "What about the waiter in the restaurant? You remember how he stared at my locket? He may have thought it was valuable. Perhaps he followed us here—" Her voice trailed off as she saw the look of incredibility on Scott's face.

"How would he be able to find out which was your room?" Scott asked doubtfully. "These village people aren't thieves. Besides," he added with vigor, "your locket is exactly where you left it when you went to bed." Her eyes widened as he continued; Scott, too, was secretly interested in her locket! "On your night table."

"You don't want to believe there was an intruder," she said faintly. She knew there was, and Scott knew there was or he wouldn't have locked the windows

and balcony with such care. She couldn't trust anyone—not even Scott.

Rosa waddled into Lisa's room with the breakfast
tray. She fussed over Lisa as though over a conva-
lescent invalid, exhorting her to rest, to eat well, not
to miss her siesta.

"Rosa, you're spoiling me," Lisa protested, sigh-
ing eloquently at the sight of the platter of Italian
sausages, the fluffy omelet, the hot rolls and the
steaming pot of coffee.

"You go home now?" Rosa prodded hopefully.
"You no like the Villa Como." Rosa knew about last
night, of course.

"I'm staying, Rosa," Lisa said softly, wishing she
dared to confide in the one person at the Villa Como
who might have known her mother. Correction, Lisa
thought inwardly; the contessa might have known
her mother.

"Better you go," Rosa maintained stolidly. She
was silent in disapproval as she set the food before
Lisa.

"Rosa," Lisa tried softly, "do you know who the
man might have been last night?

"*Jesu Maria!*" The old woman's eyes widened in
horror. "How I know?" Rosa left the room as if beset
by devils.

Lisa ate slowly, dwelling with as much calm as
she could muster on the events of the evening before.
She must go back to the restaurant and watch that
waiter to settle in her own mind whether or not he
was last night's intruder. Scott had made a point of
not coming into her room again when they returned

from the kitchen. She was frustrated in her determination to show him the room with the wet mud on the rug, for by morning it was already dry. And nobody had bothered to call the police, Lisa remembered. Surely the police should have been called.

Lisa dressed and went down to paint in the sequestered corner of the gardens she'd earmarked as her own. There was no sign of Seco anywhere this morning. She saw Pia's black Mercedes shooting down the road towards the gate about noon. One of the Englishwomen was reading aloud to the other two on the other side of the hedges. Their presence was oddly comforting. Lisa found herself able to concentrate on painting and enjoyed the effort.

"Signorina Kirby," Maria's voice intruded softly.

"Yes?" Lisa smiled.

"Luncheon soon on the terrace," Maria announced brightly. "You will please come?"

"Right away," Lisa promised. Should she change for lunch? No, Lisa compromised, she would simply wash up and go to the terrace as she was.

When Lisa arrived on the terrace, Maria and Rosa were both swooping down with enormous trays. Scott was still nowhere in sight, nor was Pia. Lisa wondered if there was any connection there and felt self-conscious at her curiosity. The contessa was replacing Pia at the head of the table so that the guests would not be without an official hostess . . . or was it watchdog?

"Miss Kirby, you have not yet met your fellow guests," the contessa said, her smile warmly ingratiating. "Miss Lounsbury," the contessa introduced a tall, graying blonde, whose glasses highlighted eyes that hinted of a wistful romanticism.

"I hope I didn't upset you last night," Lisa said.

"My dear, what a terrible experience for you," Miss Lounsbury sympathized, and Lisa could imagine her taking solicitous, tender care of a stray pup or an injured bird.

"Mrs. Eddy," the contessa continued, nodding towards a small, tightly corseted redhead. She had an air of curiosity about life. Her pupils probably teased her unmercifully, yet turned to her in moments of crisis, Lisa thought.

"I do hope you don't read gory mystery novels just before bedtime, Miss Kirby?" Mrs. Eddy stared earnestly.

"I won't ever again," Lisa laughed. So! They were all convinced she had had a nightmare.

"And this is Miss King," the contessa said, smiling at a "dowager duchess" type, who was seated facing the lake. The "dowager duchess" was an incurable romantic, Lisa surmised, the way she gazed sentimentally at the Italian lake.

Lunch arrived, and the conversation was borne largely by the three Englishwomen. The contessa smiled perfunctorily at regular intervals, contributing terse comments when addressed personally. Lisa toyed with the idea of hiring a car for a few days in order to drive about the village. Scott had said a car could be rented for ten dollars a day—and Americans were, in the eyes of Europeans, notably extravagant. Nobody would think anything of it. She would do something about it tomorrow, Lisa thought; right now she was still shaky from last night's experience.

"Here comes Mr. Anderson," Mrs. Eddy announced with an eager smile that suggested Scott Anderson had made a hit with the English ladies. "And Signora Menotti."

Scott and Pia were walking casually toward the table. The contessa called after Maria for places to be laid for them.

"I hitched a ride from town," Scott explained, grinning at Pia. "I took my car back to the agency and, lo and behold, I found myself a chauffeur."

"The agency would have sent you back to the villa," Pia said nonchalantly, seating herself at the table. Lisa, ever watchful, intercepted a look between Pia and the contessa. The black Mercedes had gone into town for the express purpose of driving Scott back to the villa. Why?

"Mr. Anderson came to us from five weeks in London," the contessa reported, her eyes moving slowly from Scott to the English ladies. "That makes him almost a compatriot." The contessa was exuding friendliness, yet Lisa had an uneasy feeling that the contessa was fishing.

"Oh?" Mrs. Eddy said brightly. "On business?"

"To see my publisher and work out some details about an assignment," Scott said outwardly nonchalant. But Lisa detected a slight tic in his right eyelid. She was astonished at this giveaway. For all his veneer of casual assurance, Scott was disturbed. "Now I have no more excuses not to get down to work." The Anderson charm spilled over generously, on cue, Lisa thought. 　　　　　　　　　•

"Your brother is in publishing, too, is he not, Miss

King?" the contessa asked, a glint of triumph in her eyes. "Perhaps Mr. Scott knows him?"

Scott started warily, eyes narrowed, but the need to answer was made unnecessary by the appearance of Rosa, tea tray in hand. "Ah, Rosa," he heralded her arrival with mock joyousness. "With concoctions fit for the angels!"

"You eat," Rosa exhorted, giggling in good humor. *"Multo buono!"*

Immediately after lunch Scott excused himself and disappeared. Lisa, like the others, returned to her room for the afternoon siesta. Despite the fact that she had slept late, she welcomed the lazy hours of relaxation. She dropped across the width of the bed and slept for almost an hour. She awoke completely refreshed and anxious for activity.

She walked across to the balcony, opened the door, yawned luxuriously and peered out across the sunlit expanse. She spotted a couple engaged in good-humored hi-jinks on the sand near the lake. Wrestling and laughing, the girl fell to the beach and the man dropped to his knees beside her. Lisa gasped. It was Maria and Scott. They were apparently sure that their little romp would go unnoticed at siesta time.

What was it with Scott Anderson? Must he make a play for every girl in sight? And why should it mean so much to her? Because, Lisa taunted herself painfully, in this short span of time she had managed to fall, like some wide-eyed teenager, for the ever-charming Signor Scott Anderson!

Lisa walked into the bathroom feeling the need for a shower. She tried to blot out the picture of Maria and Scott. What could Maria and Scott possibly have in common? But then Maria was most attractive, in a young animal fashion, Lisa compelled herself to be honest; and Scott Anderson was a completely normal male. Scott had made the rounds: Pia Menotti, Maria, and herself! All right, Lisa promised herself, after this, Scott would find her not quite so eager. So sure of himself, she thought, simmering. She would show him!

As she dressed, a plan formed in her mind. The bus stopped just outside the villa. She could hop a bus into town and drop into the restaurant for an ice. If anyone questioned her reasons . . . well, she was a crazy American who had to be doing things. She made mental notes: pick up the papers; stop by the post office for stamps; decide once and for all whether the waiter at the restaurant was the man who had crept into her room last night.

Lisa learned that the one afternoon bus to town would be passing the villa at any moment. The girl on the phone sounded astonished that anyone would be interested in leaving the villa at this time of day. Lisa sprinted through the deserted house to the door, and down the steps to the gate.

She was perspiring by the time she arrived at the gates. She let herself out remembering that at dusk these gates would be locked again. She walked, trying not to think about Scott lying on the white sand beside Maria, who had been so frank in her invitations from the moment she had laid eyes on Scott.

The bus came along and pulled to a stop. The driver grinned as she scrambled aboard. The bus was deserted except for an elderly woman snoring on a rear seat. Lisa made her way to a seat, holding on as she walked. The driver was suddenly in a rush to make up time. She had made one mistake, Lisa chastised herself; she had spoken to the driver in fluent Italian. He had even congratulated her for knowing the language. No more missteps like that!

In less than ten minutes the bus deposited her on the main street. She saw the canopy of the restaurant where they had dined the night before. Feeling strange in the near-empty streets, she paused and decided to pick up the papers first. There was a café on the lake. She would have an ice there at one of the outside tables, she decided, then go into the restaurant for coffee.

Lisa sat at a small table under an awning, slowly eating her lemon ice. A black car moved down the street and Lisa snapped to attention. It was a black Mercedes, with a man behind the wheel. Lisa leaned forward, squinting for a better look. But the distance was too great for her to recognize the driver. It *was* the car from the villa, Lisa realized with excitement, remembering that a blob of green lay across the rear window. A green cashmere sweater of Pia's that Lisa had seen there before. Her hunch had been right! She spent several moments speculating about who the driver was. Then the car turned left, fading from view, leaving Lisa disappointed.

As Lisa paid for the lemon ice she resolved to go into the restaurant immediately to look at the waiter. And if she decided he was the man, what then? Her heart pounded as she considered the situation. Call the police? What proof did she have? Her word against the waiter's. The contessa would be furious; she might even be asked to leave the villa.

En route to the restaurant Lisa stopped in a small shop to buy a package of cigarettes, though she seldom smoked, then on impulse bought a tin of pipe tobacco. She stuffed both into her purse and headed with mounting nervousness for the restaurant. Suppose the man confronted her? How could she tell what he might do?

The restaurant was dark and deserted as she entered, and for an instant she was afraid. But the rotund, bejeweled woman she remembered from the day before came forward now and ushered Lisa to a table. If the woman were surprised to see Lisa here again, alone, she managed to conceal it admirably.

"Just coffee, please," Lisa stammered. "Coffee— and cookies or a pastry." She made a point of mispronouncing the Italian, smiling in apology at her ineptness.

"*Si, signorina,*" the woman smiled in return as she trotted off to the kitchen.

Lisa gazed about with apprehension. The women appeared to be alone in the restaurant. She should have realized the waiter might have been on duty only in the evening. Was the waiter someone known to the Menottis, Lisa questioned herself? Was it the locket he was seeking in her room, or something else? Again, Lisa recalled the tin of tobacco Pia had brought back from Milan on the day of her arrival. A tobacco probably unattainable in the village here. Bought for whom?

The woman returned with a tray and placed the coffee and pastry before Lisa.

"*Torcetti,*" the woman said, pointing to the twin

crescents on the plate. "Pastry," she explained in reply to Lisa's polite blank smile.

The woman took her place behind the cash register, her eyes regularly checking the entrance. All at once, she walked swiftly to the door and spoke urgently in a rapid-fire Italian that Lisa found difficult to hear. A man on the other side of the door was hidden by the frame. The woman was telling him not to come into the restaurant, to go away until later. "The girl is here," Lisa heard the woman explain nervously.

Lisa pretended to be absorbed by the pastry. She noted that the man was leaving and the woman, with relief returned to her perch behind the cash register. Almost at the same moment, Scott appeared in the doorway. He peered inside, spied her, and walked to her table.

"Pretend you were expecting me," Scott said under his breath. "We're a pair of screwball American tourists."

"What took you so long, Scott?" Lisa demanded loudly, the tension in her voice passing for annoyance. "I've been here almost ten minutes." He had seen the man at the door. Was it their waiter of last night? Why would the woman order him away, unless he were the intruder?

"I wanted to get some film for the camera," Scott said, and gestured to the woman for service.

For a few moments they discussed what Scott would have, then the woman disappeared again into the kitchen.

"You little idiot!" Scott reproached under his

breath. "I had a hunch you were pulling off something like this!"

"The man at the door," Lisa whispered, gazing apprehensively towards the kitchen. "Was it the waiter?"

"Yes," Scott said somberly. "In quite a hurry to get away."

"The woman told him to leave," Lisa reported, her breathing strained. "Not to come back for at least two hours. I heard her. She said: 'The girl is here'— meaning me, I gather!"

"Since when do you understand Italian?" Scott asked with astonishment.

"Since I was a child," Lisa confessed. "My mother was an American but she loved Italian. She made a point of seeing that I learned the language."

"Sharp of you to keep it a secret," he acknowledged.

"What do I do now?" Lisa asked. "About the waiter?"

"Nothing," Scott sighed. "We have nothing the police would accept as evidence." He was silent a moment, brows furrowed in thought. "What are you doing at the villa, Lisa?" he demanded bluntly. "What mad chase brought you here just now?"

"My mother was killed in an accident two months ago," Lisa said, with disarming simplicity. "Just before she died, she begged me to come to Italy, to see the country she loved so much. I discovered the Villa Como through a travel agency." Her eyes couldn't quite manage to meet Scott's.

"That's all?" he pursued, skeptical.

"What else could there be?" She forced her eyes to meet his guilelessly.

"I don't know," Scott sighed. "But when I saw you from the terrace, trotting along to the bus, I got this crazy hunch you were going after trouble. I dreamt up an excuse to borrow the Mercedes." His eyes traveled to her neckline. "You're not wearing the locket today."

"Oh yes," Lisa whispered, tugging at the chain so that Scott could see the locket nestled beneath the neckline.

"Did you say your father brought that back from Italy?" Scott squinted in thought.

"That's right." Lisa was conscious of her heart pounding against her ribs. There was too much about Scott that she didn't know, Lisa warned herself. She must not confide in him.

"Hardly seems the sort of thing a man would risk breaking into a villa to steal," Scott pointed out.

"I'm sure it's of no value," Lisa insisted. "I can't imagine why he wanted it." Only the waiter would know that, she thought with frustration.

"Of course, the man may be nothing more than a petty thief," Scott conceded.

Lisa felt that Scott shared her conviction that there was some deeper significance to the attempted robbery. At least Scott agreed with her that the man had been in her room after the locket. That knowledge was reassuring. Why had the waiter risked a jail sentence for this locket? What meaning did it hold that she was unable to interpret?

"When you're in a mood to talk," Scott said softly, "I'll be waiting to listen."

They did not talk about the episode in the restaurant as they drove back to the villa. Scott was making a determined effort to throw off the somber mood that had overtaken them both. Lisa kept recalling his romp on the beach with Maria; she was jealous that the Anderson charm was spread about so generously.

Once, as they swung around a sharp curve, Lisa fell against Scott and stayed close to him for a moment. She felt an answering response in Scott though his conversation remained good-naturedly casual. Too many secrets between them, Lisa thought wistfully.

They arrived at the villa, which was still entrenched in its afternoon quiet. Lisa returned to her room while Scott took off, presumably to garage the car. But even an hour later, there were still no sounds in his room that would indicate he had come upstairs.

At dinner Lisa arrived at the table to find that Scott was not there. She fought down her disappointment.

Mrs. Eddy, who was dressed in a violently floral print, looked about with bright-eyed curiosity. "Where is the charming Mr. Anderson?" Mrs. Eddy turned to the contessa. "Are we to be completely female this evening?"

"I'm afraid so," the contessa smiled. Her eyes regarded Mrs. Eddy's print silk with obvious distaste. It was so in contrast with the severe black she herself wore. "Mr. Anderson had an engagement elsewhere."

Where was Scott, Lisa wondered as she kept up a

gay conversation with Miss King about the difficulties of making oneself understood in foreign countries. Lisa was ashamed of the wave of jealousy that flooded her when she considered that Scott might be off somewhere with Maria. Then her jealousy was supplanted by alarm because she remembered that Scott, too, traveled under false colors. What was he after here at the Villa Como? Was he in danger right this minute? Scott would not be the type to retreat before trouble.

Lisa told herself later that she was not unable to sleep merely because Scott had not returned. She was overtired, too keyed up to sleep. The night winds continued to unnerve her. Twice, she checked the windows and the balcony doors when normally she would never think of locking them. She buried her face in one of the deep pillows, pulled the bedclothes over her head. Sleep! Why was it so elusive?

For the next three days Lisa found herself in the company of the three Englishwomen much of the time. They adopted a warm, solicitous attitude towards her. Lisa guessed that they were developing romantic ideas about Scott and her. Scott put in fleeting appearances at dinner. He seemed absentminded and engrossed in some personal project. One day he drove into Milan to have his typewriter repaired—or so he said.

Lisa was growing restless with frustration at the lack of answers to the questions that plagued her. Scott had conscientiously avoided her eyes as he talked at dinner about his trip into Milan. He discussed the problems of having a part imported for replacement in the typewriter which, of course, provided him with an alibi for another trip into Milan. She was getting nowhere, Lisa reproached herself. Even Rosa had retreated into a taciturn watchfulness. The silent clashes between Pia and the contessa hinted at an uneasy truce between the two women. It was as though all of them at the Villa Como were sitting on the edge of a volcano, waiting for it to erupt.

That night as Lisa settled into bed, she promised herself not to lie awake again until the darkness gave way to gray. Tonight, inspecting herself in the mirror, _she noted with distaste shadows beneath her eyes and a look of tiredness. Why play games with herself? She was anxious to be attractive for Scott. She was eager to have him look at her and find her desirable. No man had ever stirred her quite the way Scott did. Finally, after much shuffling around beneath the comforter, searching for a position conducive to sleep, Lisa drifted off into chaotic dreams that centered around Scott and herself, in which they eluded disaster by seconds, racing hand in hand through the dark night.

And then all at once she was awake, conscious of sounds in the garden below. First it was Scott's voice raised in fury; then a scuffle and a groan.

Lisa rushed to the balcony. Her hands were trembling so that she could barely unlock the door. In the garden below, she could see Scott lying face down with Obermann and Pia hovering over him.

"You idiot, Carl!" Pia hissed in Italian. "What have you done now?"

SEVEN

Lisa gripped the balcony railing, her eyes wide in terror as she watched the tableau in the garden below. Pia was on her knees beside Scott, tugging at his shoulders in an effort to swing him over onto his back while Carl Obermann scowled above them.

"What is it?" Lisa gasped, her voice shrill in the night silence. "What's happened to Scott?"

Pia looked up, startled, and shot a swift warning glance at Obermann before she spoke.

"A small accident, Miss Kirby," she said, keeping her voice low. "Nothing to worry about. Please go back into your room before you disturb the others."

Lisa whirled about, rushed across her room and out the door, conscious only of the fact that Scott was hurt and that in some way Carl Obermann was responsible. She ran noiselessly down the corridor, holding the folds of her robe above her ankles so that her speed would not be impeded. Breathlessly, she arrived at the foot of the staircase in time to see Carl Obermann, with Scott slung across his shoulder, coming through a side door. Pia followed close behind him.

Pia grew angry when she spotted Lisa. "Miss Kirby, I thought I asked you to remain in your room!"

"You have no right to issue orders to me at a time

like this," Lisa blazed, no longer afraid, only concerned for Scott. "I want to know what's happened to Scott!"

"He is merely stunned," Carl Obermann announced reassuringly. "Pia, bring hot water, antiseptic, cotton, and a towel." Pia hesitated, still staring at Lisa. "Pia, get water and a towel, please," Carl ordered with authority.

"Take him to the small library in the rear," Pia said. She lifted her head imperiously but she was retreating.

"What happened?" Lisa tried again, running to keep up with Carl's huge strides as he charged through a series of open doors. She noted that Obermann was thoroughly familiar with the layout of the villa.

"An unfortunate mistake, for which I am most regretful." He panted slightly beneath the weight of Scott's body. "But please, Miss Kirby, do not be upset." His eyes met hers with quiet solicitude, which astonished Lisa because she remembered the brusque, almost brutal quality she felt in the man before. "We will bring him around in a few minutes."

Lisa hovered unhappily over Scott as Obermann deposited him on the sofa. Then she realized they were in the tiny room where the contessa had come upon her with such indignation.

"He's so still," Lisa said, shivering.

"Pulse is normal," Obermann reported. "There is a very slight laceration of the scalp. His jaw, I fear, will be painful for a day or two," he said in apology.

In the back of her mind, disturbed as she was, Lisa noticed that Obermann seemed familiar with medical terms. Lisa relaxed slightly, feeling an odd confidence in Obermann's presence. She looked around the room and once again studied the portrait on the wall. Astonishing, how that face continued to haunt her!

"We must be quiet," Pia reminded them as she walked into the room and closed the door behind her.

Pia's eyes clashed with Lisa's and were darkly hostile, communicating a silent threat. She placed the basin of water on the floor beside the sofa, then dipped the towel into it. Handing a bottle of antiseptic to Carl, she waited while he applied the antiseptic to the surface laceration.

"I think Miss Kirby appreciates the need for quiet," he murmured, busy with the bottle of antiseptic. "I do not think we need even to clip the hair," he decided with satisfaction. He reached for the towel Pia held in readiness and placed it behind Scott's neck. "It was really such an absurd accident. I have been on duty at the villa to make sure there would be no trespassing, as has been happening in the area—"

"Which is why we were so certain no one could have entered your room last night," Pia pounced in triumph. "Because we have arranged for Carl to patrol the grounds every night since there has been trouble." Lisa guessed that Pia deliberately used Signor Obermann's first name, to make it clear that their relationship was personal. "No one could have been here without Carl knowing it. We have been silent so as not to disturb our guests."

"Mr. Anderson must have been taking a late walk about the grounds," Carl explained. "Close to three in the morning," he pointed out. "I could only presume he was a trespasser." Carl made no speculation as to why Scott was prowling about the grounds at three in the morning. Undoubtedly, both Carl and Pia were as curious as she about Scott's motives.

Scott stirred. As he moved his head to one side, he groaned.

"Easy," Obermann advised. "That was, I regret, a nasty crack that brought you down."

Scott's eyes opened slowly. "What the devil?" He tried to sit up, swore under his breath.

"In a few minutes," Obermann encouraged, gently pushing Scott back. "When I ran into you in the dark, at this hour, I naturally assumed you were the intruder Miss Kirby professed to see last night."

"There was no intruder," Pia flashed back.

"Of course not," Carl agreed smoothly, "but for the moment I thought I might have been careless the night before. Sorry for that crack on the jaw, Mr. Anderson."

"Shouldn't we phone for a doctor?" Lisa suggested uneasily.

"No need," Scott reassured, reaching to squeeze her hand. "I've been hit harder before."

"I am sure a good night's sleep will be all Mr. Anderson requires," Obermann said. Lisa sensed his relief—and Pia's—that Scott had rejected medical assistance.

As Scott began slowly to edge himself into a sitting position, he glanced about the room. His eyes fastened to the painting on the wall. His mouth seemed, to Lisa, to tighten as he stared at the picture of the young boy. Lisa spied the look of apprehension that passed from Pia to Carl. The room was suddenly heavy with unspoken conjectures. Pia was white about the mouth, her eyes sharply intent on Scott's reactions.

"Handsome youngster," Scott commented casually. "Member of the family?"

"A young cousin," Pia said carelessly, some of her tension seeming to evaporate.

"You could probably use a drink," Carl suggested. "Pia, bring in a bottle, please."

"Yes," Pia said reluctantly and walked swiftly from the room.

Carl Obermann was not playing the role of a man hired to guard the villa against trespassers now, Lisa noticed. But, of course, it was fairly clear that Carl and Pia were lovers. Again, Lisa wondered why the contessa permitted the presence about the villa of someone she obviously disliked. Or was it that she disliked Carl Obermann for replacing her dead son?

Lisa sensed that Scott was making a strong effort not to stare at the picture. Pia had said the portrait was that of a young cousin; the contessa had identified the dark-haired, blue-eyed youngster as her stepson. Who was lying, and why?

Questions were piling up in Lisa's mind, with the answers frustratingly not at hand. But at least Scott was all right, she thought, in relief. She watched as the two men drank the whiskey Pia brought in. They talked casually as though this were some social occasion. She didn't want to think what it would mean to her if Scott had been injured badly.

Lisa breakfasted on the balcony, aware of the companion balcony that jutted forth from Scott's room. He would probably sleep till lunch, she thought regretfully, yearning for a reassuring sight of him. Maybe she ought to have insisted on having a doctor called in, she chided herself uneasily.

Though she was finished with breakfast, she was reluctant to stir from the balcony which seemed to bring her closer to Scott. It was another glorious summer day. Out on the far side of the lake, two sailboats skimmed across the water.

There was a sound on the next balcony. Someone was fumbling with the shuttered doors. Lisa waited expectantly for Scott to appear.

"How do you feel?" she asked solicitously as Scott, in dressing gown, hair tumbled from sleep, stepped out into the late morning sunlight.

"The head's still there," he grimaced expressively. "Tough, I guess."

"I was scared to death for a few minutes," Lisa said candidly.

"I'll be in no mood for work till this head clears. What do you say we go sightseeing? I can phone down to the village for a car."

"Do you think you should?" But the prospect of another day alone with Scott was enticing.

"Why not?" he said exuberantly. "There's another little town around the other end of the lake that I hear is real tourist bait," he coaxed.

"Does Maria have a relative with a restaurant there, too?" she jibed.

"Maria has relatives all over the place," he grinned. "Nothing like having a contact in the restaurants. We'll skip lunch here," Scott planned. "Eat in town."

"If you're sure," Lisa agreed after a slight hesitation.

"Stop worrying about me," Scott kidded, a satisfied glow in his eyes for the moment. "I'm rugged." The gaze became contemplative, serious as it dwelt on Lisa. "Besides, I want a chance to talk to you."

Her breath quickened in anticipation. "Yes?"

"Not here," Scott rejected. "I'll phone down for a car. At the rate of speed the characters in the village operate, we ought to have a car up here in two hours. Until it comes, I'll be sleeping in a chaise down on the terrace."

"I'll collect you later," Lisa promised. She wondered why he wanted to talk to her away from the villa. She remembered Scott's face when his eyes lingered on that portrait of the boy . . . it was startled, intense. Was that boy her stepbrother? Was he in danger? Was that Scott's reason for being at the Villa Como?

From her painting corner, Lisa spied a gray Fiat come to a stop in the driveway. A man dressed in a blue suit and sporting a mustache climbed out and approached the villa entrance. She could hear the sound of voices without being able to distinguish what was said. Then the man reappeared and walked nimbly down the stairs, probably heading for a bus ride back into town.

She wound up her morning's painting pleased with her efforts. With the easel and paints in tow, she walked leisurely back to the house. It would take her no more than ten minutes to change and come back downstairs to pick up Scott. What did he want to talk to her about? Lisa asked herself again with a return of disquiet.

When Lisa strolled back out to the side terrace,

Scott was sprawled on the chaise, ostensibly asleep. It would be unkind to wake him, she decided, flooded by tenderness.

"Good morning," Carl Obermann's voice startled her. He was walking up the steps of the terrace. "I hope you slept well for the rest of the night?"

"Oh, yes," she said quickly. It was astonishing, this complete about-face of Obermann. How different from the man who had hovered so menacingly above her on the terrace last week! He was smiling, almost gentle, and candidly admiring her. "Scott seems to be catching up, too," she laughed. Carl Obermann was now an accepted member of the household, Lisa assumed, not as displeased as she might have been a week ago.

"I've caught up," Scott announced, opening his eyes. Lisa saw the look of dislike he shot in Carl's direction. "The car's arrived."

"I'm ready," Lisa said, conscious of Carl's scrutiny as he lowered himself into a chair and scrounged in his pocket for cigarettes. "Oh, I did the craziest thing the other day," she laughed, watching both men. "I went to the tobacco shop for cigarettes—" She was aware of the quick look Scott gave her—he had never seen her smoke; she would have to make a point of smoking after dinner. "And the man must have given me someone else's parcel because there was pipe tobacco inside. Either of you pipe smokers?" she asked with an attempt at guilelessness.

"Not I," Scott said briefly.

"Nor I," Carl answered as his eyes traveled the slender length of Lisa in her summery turquoise cotton. "Though I know you American women find pipe-smoking romantic." Carl's eyes held Lisa's, telling her that he found her most attractive as she stood there with the sunlight on her pert young face. Lisa caught the look of frank annoyance on Scott's face.

"Come on," Scott said tersely. "Let's go."

He put a hand possessively at her elbow and moved her toward the stairs. Lisa smiled and waved at Carl to hide her embarrassment; Scott had been almost rude. He was probably still remembering the clout on the jaw last night, Lisa conceded—but Carl had explained that. Though he had never explained his belligerency when they had wandered in the vicinity of the closed left wing of the villa. What was that bit the contessa had tossed at them, about his being here to check on the safety of the other wing?

As they settled themselves in the car, Lisa sensed that Carl Obermann was watching them. The car bolted ahead jolting Lisa toward the dashboard. Swearing under his breath, Scott shot a hand forward to catch her and smiled in apology. Looking back, Lisa thought she saw Pia Menotti walk out onto the terrace and stand beside Carl.

"We'll give this other town a look," Scott said, keeping his eyes on the road ahead and driving more swiftly than usual.

"Let's get there in one piece," she laughed, catching at the side of the car as it squealed round another curve in the road.

"Worried?" He glanced solicitously in her direction.

"No." She was aware that her heart was pounding, that whatever Scott said to her she would believe, that she wished right this moment he would stop the car and kiss her.

"That's my girl," he crooned, letting one hand

leave the wheel for an instant to close about hers.

That was one of the things about Scott that set him apart for her, made him special, Lisa thought with a surge of pleasure—his delightful warmth and compassion. She felt that to be loved by Scott Anderson would be to be loved with all the intensity of which one man was capable. Yet wasn't she jumping, Lisa warned herself? Scott had in no way committed himself, except in these little attentions which she might be misreading because she wished so desperately to believe that he was in love with her.

They drove in silence the rest of the way, both caught up in private thoughts. The town at the far end of the lake was small, picturesque, and dotted with appealing little shops. Because it was close to siesta time, activity in the town was almost at a standstill. They found the restaurant Scott had chosen, on Maria's advice, and walked inside. Only a pair of patrons still dawdled over lunch. A small, dark, sturdily built waitress walked over to serve them, radiating good humor.

"You order," Lisa said quickly.

"Trusting one," he jibed, but concentrated on the menu while the waitress waited. *"Risotta alla Milanese,"* he decided, "with a salad—*fennel,* I believe. *Taleggio.* Iced coffee."

"A bottle of Grumello?" the waitress enticed.

"Grumello," he accepted, with a wink at Lisa, "lest we be considered uncivilized." Scott leaned back, pleased that the ordering was out of the way.

"May I have a cigarette?" Lisa asked when the waitress left them.

"I didn't know you smoked," Scott smiled, reaching for the pack.

"Carl Obermann said that he doesn't smoke a pipe," Lisa remarked, trying to sound casual.

"So?" Scott lifted an eyebrow inquiringly as he leaned forward with his cigarette lighter.

"The night Pia Menotti picked us up at the Milan airport," Lisa said quietly, "she also stopped off to buy a tin of pipe tobacco. I saw it in her pocket when we reached the villa."

"It's a cinch neither the contessa nor she smoke a pipe," Scott conceded. "Nor, apparently, does Carl Obermann." His eyes glowed with a sudden intensity.

"You don't like him," Lisa said softly.

"Like who?" Scott dodged, his eyes on the immaculate white tablecloth.

"Obermann," Lisa said with a show of impatience.

"He hasn't exactly endeared himself to me," Scott acknowledged. "I have a natural dislike of men who prowl around with German Lugers at their waist."

"He told you about the prowlers in the neighborhood," Lisa reminded.

"Sure," Scott said crisply, almost angrily.

"What were you doing roaming about at that hour of the night, anyway?" Lisa asked, making an effort to sound amused.

"I couldn't sleep. I went for a walk." His face tightened. "Then that storm trooper came at me."

"Scott," Lisa reproved gently.

"I think you ought to get away from the villa," Scott said quietly.

"Why?" she challenged. "You're the second person to come at me with that—" She stopped, but it was too late to cover her slip.

"Who else?" Scott demanded swiftly. "Well?" he prodded when she was silent.

"Rosa," Lisa said. "She wouldn't say why."

"When are you going to level with me, Lisa?" Scott challenged.

"Why can't you believe I'm an art student here for a summer of painting?" she persisted. "Is that so fantastic?" Scott was right; why couldn't she level with him?

"You keep looking around for ghosts," Scott scolded.

"I'd say *your* camouflage is rough around the edges," she tossed out with a show of bravado.

"Like what?" He was calm but waiting intently for her answer.

"Like the way you type," she listed. "You keep hitting the same letter repeatedly, to give the impression of typing."

"Bright girl," he commented. "Go on."

"The way you dodged when Miss King was talking about her brother in publishing, in London, where you were supposed to have been for five weeks."

"You didn't buy that?"

"Your luggage was new, no labels anywhere, yet you had been in London for five weeks and before that in Mexico."

"That's all?" he asked, seemingly relieved.

"The way you looked at that fake Modigliani and knew it for what it was. The way you looked at the painting of the boy in the little rear room last night." She was faintly breathless, her eyes purple with excitement, feeling herself close to something. "Scott, you know that boy," she said urgently. "Who is he?"

"I thought you might have known," he said cautiously. "There was something about the way you looked at the painting—"

"I don't know," Lisa insisted impatiently. "I felt for a moment as if I knew him. It might be a passing resemblance to someone else."

"A striking resemblance," Scott agreed. "That's what bothered me from the beginning! From the moment I saw you standing there at the airport. It didn't hit me until last night, looking at the painting —and you." His hand tightened on the wheel. "It's astonishing!"

"What is astonishing?" Lisa demanded, leaning towards him, her eyes ablaze.

"Look in your purse mirror, Lisa," Scott ordered gently. "I don't know what wind blew you here, but you're caught up right in the middle of one gigantic mess."

"The boy in the painting," Lisa whispered, her eyes wide as she groped with reality. "My brother! I really have a brother." Her voice was low with the miracle of discovery that there was someone so close to her.

"So that's why you're at the Villa Como," Scott said softly. "I saw it in your eyes, that look of searching, waiting for something to happen. Lisa, what do you know about Tony?"

"Tony?" Excitement flooded her. Her brother Tony! "Is that his name, Scott?"

"The man in the picture is Tony Menotti," Scott began.

"Man?" Lisa interrupted, a dozen questions crowding together in her mind. "I thought he was a child!"

"Tony's close to thirty. The portrait was painted many years ago by his father."

"*My* father," Lisa whispered, taking pride in the sudden realization that he had been an accomplished artist. "My mother was a WAC—she stayed here at the Villa Como. Scott, who is Tony? Who am I?" The contessa said the boy in the portrait was her stepson; Pia had identified him as a young cousin.

"I thought you knew," Scott said, startled. "Tony Menotti is Pia's husband, the contessa's stepson."

"But Pia said her husband was dead!" Lisa exclaimed in shock.

"That's the bilge they threw at me," Scott acknowledged grimly. "I've been terribly disturbed about Tony—he disappeared from Paris five weeks ago, without a word to me, his closest friend. I had just been back from Mexico a month. Tony didn't tell me that he was married until I popped into the studio that first day back. Pia was out and he made a point of hustling me out before she returned. They got married on a lost weekend in Milan ten months ago; Tony knew it was a mistake right away, but Pia was sure she had latched onto money. The villa belongs to Tony—he had been making plans to turn it into a sanctuary for impoverished artists. I understand both Pia and the contessa were furious."

"Scott, where is Tony?" Lisa's eyes were dark with fear. "What's happened to him?"

"That's why I'm here," Scott explained with quiet determination. "To find Tony. Two weeks ago, I received a peculiar cable calling for help. He said to come to the villa and to keep my reason secret. It was signed 'Tony' but gave a fictitious last name and an address here in town. Lisa, you must help me! We have to find Tony before it's too late!"

"You think he's here at the villa?"

"He has to be," Scott said urgently. "Pray that Tony is here, Lisa!"

EIGHT

The waitress was putting their food on the table. Lisa tapped her foot impatiently, wishing the waitress would finish, wanting to know more.

"Scott, what do we do now?" Lisa asked when they were at last alone again. "Can't we go to the police?"

"The local *carabinieri?*" Scott smiled wryly. "How far would we get? The contessa is an important figure in the towns about the villa; we'd get nowhere. Besides, what have we got to go on?"

"The cable," Lisa reminded.

"With a fictitious last name and address?" Scott shook his head. "We would be a pair of hysterical Americans. Besides, we can't take a chance on forcing their hand."

"You believe the contessa and Pia are working together to prevent Tony from turning the villa into an artists' haven?" Lisa asked fearfully. She couldn't bring herself to say, "to kill Tony".

Scott nodded. "The two women and Obermann. But there must be something much deeper involved —I can't quite get the pitch yet." His eyes studied her at length. "Suppose you fill me in on your side, Lisa."

"I told you about—about my mother's accident." It was still difficult for her to talk about her mother's death without emotion. "Everything happened so terribly fast. Those last few minutes in the hospital when she told me to come here. She warned me not to let anyone know who I was. Her last words were—" Lisa's voice dropped to a whisper and her eyes filled with tears. "Be careful, darling. Danger. Much danger. Find your brother. Find what belongs to you—"

"I figure there has to be something else." Scott's eyes narrowed thoughtfully. "Something at the villa which neither you nor I know about." His eyes returned to her again, showing his unease. "Lisa, I want you to get out of here. Tonight, if possible!"

"No," Lisa insisted. "I have to help. Why were you prowling last night?"

"I was hoping to see some sign of life in the closed wing of the villa. Obermann cut me down before I had a chance. I'll have to try again—when he's inside the villa with the others. It should be easier, now that he's not under cover."

"Scott, be careful!"

"Don't worry so much," he chided with a show of humor.

"You've been here at the villa before," she guessed. "With Tony?"

"For a weekend two years ago. The contessa was in Paris. Tony's made a point of being away as much as possible, practically altogether these last two years. There's little love lost between Tony and his stepmother."

"Tell me about Tony," Lisa begged impulsively. "I know so little about anything."

"Tony is marvelous," Scott said affectionately. "Warm, talented, handsome as the devil. He would give his last nickel to somebody in trouble. You're a lot alike I think," he said quietly, and a pinkness colored Lisa's cheeks. "The contessa was Mario Menotti's second wife, of course. The first wife died in childbirth."

"Mario?" Lisa repeated, eyes bright with wonder. "My father's name was Mario?"

"An artist, like Tony and you," Scott smiled.

"And yourself," Lisa pounced, eyes watching him tenderly, daring him to deny this.

"You can see why I was so anxious to keep it secret."

"What happened to my father?" Lisa pursued.

"He was killed by the Nazis towards the end of the war. He had been with the underground from the very beginning, fighting against fascism. The old contessa, your grandmother, died at the hands of the Fascists. Tony saw her taken away. She was a wonderful old lady, Tony says. The Villa Como was willed to him, but the present contessa was in control until he reached twenty-eight."

"And now that he wants to take over, they're trying to stop him!" Lisa guessed in agitation. "Scott, what do we do?"

Scott looked at his watch. "I have to make a phone call to Paris in ten minutes," he admitted. "I have a friend checking on Obermann. That was why I went into Milan—after what happened with that slimy waiter, I wasn't taking chances on a telephone leakage."

"Where does he fit in?" Lisa prodded.

"I can't figure it," Scott said frankly, "except that somehow your locket belongs in this picture. Maybe if Tony saw it, he would understand. Maybe it was just coincidence, a thief mistaking the locket for something valuable. We won't know about that, honey, until we find Tony."

"What do you expect to find out about Obermann?" Lisa asked, then was silent because the waitress returned to their table with coffee.

"I don't know, Lisa," Scott admitted somberly. "I'm hoping there'll be something in the report to guide us." He pushed his chair back. "Wait here for me. I'll go into the hotel down the street to make the phone call. Stay here," he repeated.

"Where would I go?" Lisa smiled. "You're buying my lunch."

Lisa settled back, sipped her coffee and tried to assimilate the wealth of information Scott had poured out to her. Suddenly, she had a whole family: a grandmother, a father, a brother. Her mother must have known about her father's death, Lisa decided. Why had she warned against danger? Why the secrecy? *What* belonged to Lisa?

She sat forward, clutching at the cup of steaming coffee as though it might provide answers. She tensed suddenly as she recognized a couple walking in the street outside. Pia Menotti and Carl Obermann! What were they doing here? Going to a hotel together? Hardly. The town was too close to the villa, they might be seen.

Lisa deliberated for a moment, then on impulse reached for her purse and signalled urgently to the waitress.

"I will return," Lisa said in fluent Italian that took the waitress by surprise. "Tell the signor to wait here for me, please." She dug about in her purse for money to pay the check.

Lisa walked out into the hot afternoon sun, quickly spying the pair from the villa. They were separating now. Carl crossed the street to a small gift shop. Pia looked down the near-empty street, as though aware of eyes upon her, and Lisa darted nervously into a fruit stall. She dawdled for a few moments and bought some oranges. Then, determined to learn Pia's objective in town, she walked with outward casualness along the street. She spotted Pia in the apothecary at the corner and walked inside, butterflies in the pit of her stomach. Lisa searched quickly for an alibi for her presence; in her wallet, was a prescription for sleeping pills that she had been given by the family doctor after her mother's death. A prescription which she had kept with her these tedious weeks.

Lisa walked to the back of the shop, anticipating the startled look in Pia's flashing eyes when they would light on her. "Hello," Lisa said calmly. For once she had the upper hand, she felt. "We seem to have a common destination today."

Pia was tense and annoyed. "I understood you were to have a day of sightseeing—with Signor Anderson."

"We're having lunch down the street," Lisa reported, aware that Pia was discomfited by her presence. What was the druggist preparing for Pia back behind those shelves? "I decided to run down and have a prescription filled." She guessed now, belatedly, that Pia was suspicious that Lisa had followed her. "Sleeping pills," Lisa confided. "I use them now and then when I have trouble sleeping."

"Yes, many Americans resort to such," Pia smiled with a touch of the familiar condescension.

Pia's face brightened as the druggist returned. She listened politely while he explained in Italian that he would have to order from Milan one of the drugs she had requested. It would take a few days to arrive.

"I would appreciate a swift delivery," Pia told him crisply. "These are for a guest who is a chemist—he wishes to experiment."

There was no guest at the villa who was a chemist, Lisa thought angrily. What kind of drugs was Pia ordering; for whom? Terror welled in her, making her fingers unsteady as she pulled the prescription from her wallet and held it towards the druggist. Were Pia and Carl in a conspiracy to poison her brother? How could Scott and she remain quiet now? They must go to the police!

"I hope Signor Anderson and you have an interesting day," Pia said with an odd smile. "You will be back at the villa for dinner?"

"We expect to be," Lisa said uncertainly, wishing Pia would leave so that she could be done with this play-acting and hurry back to the restaurant. Scott would be furious with her for leaving.

Lisa waited for her prescription to be filled, wishing she dared to question the druggist about Pia's purchase. But when the small bottle was handed to her, she simply paid for it and hurried out into the street. People were beginning to appear along the street, mostly tourists, peering into the shop windows. No sign of Pia Menotti now, or of Carl Obermann.

Scott was at their table. He had ordered iced coffee for both of them again, and the waitress was serving it as Lisa hurried back to him.

"Did you get your call through?" Lisa asked breathlessly, waiting for the waitress to leave.

"Yes," Scott nodded, noncommittal, his eyes warning her not to speak until they were alone.

"I remembered a prescription I wanted to fill," Lisa lied for the benefit of the curious waitress. "I saw the apothecary at the corner." The waitress trailed away to disappear behind the door that led to the kitchen.

"What do you mean running off that way?" Scott scolded heatedly. "You scared hell out of me!"

"I saw Pia and Carl Obermann," Lisa said softly. "They walked right by here."

"You followed them?" Anxiety kindled in Scott's eyes.

"I thought we might learn something," Lisa said. "Carl went over to a gift shop, Pia into the apothecary. I don't know what she ordered, but there was something the man said he would have to get from Milan. I gathered it'll take a few days. Pia gave him some story about having a guest who's a chemist." She watched him worriedly for reaction.

"God!" Scott's hand tightened into a fist, his face set. "That means in the next few days, before Pia comes back to the drugstore, we have to find Tony!"

"Scott, can't we go to the police?" Lisa pleaded.

"I'm afraid of what'll happen to Tony." Lisa realized how easily the name of her brother came to her lips now, as though he had always been a part of her life.

Scott shook his head tiredly. "We have nothing to give the police, Lisa—except suspicious coincidences. And we can't afford to push their hand, not until we know where Tony is."

"The closed wing?" Lisa frowned in thought. "Scott, he has to be there!" And then she remembered Scott's phone call. "What did you find out, when you phoned Paris?"

"I have a line on Obermann," Scott admitted evasively.

"What about him?" Lisa's eyes clung to his face.

"The report isn't complete yet," Scott acknowledged, "but the way I get the picture Carl Obermann was a Nazi who was a staff member at a concentration camp. After the war he disappeared for years, was suspected of being in South America for a while, then Paris."

"You think that's where Pia met him?" Lisa asked, her mind searching avidly for connecting links.

"It's possible. I dug up some more on the Menottis," he added, distaste clouding his face. "The present contessa, the report says, was a friend of the Fascists. During the war she was suspected of sleeping regularly with Nazi officers. Of course, when the tide of the war turned," he said ironically, "the contessa switched affections."

"But didn't the people in the villages here know that?" Lisa demanded, remembering that the Menottis were regarded with the greatest respect.

"The people in the village knew only of Mario, who

was a partisan leader, and the old contessa who died in the Fascist prison."

"My father and my grandmother," Lisa said with a wistful pride. "I wish I could have known them!"

"You'll know Tony," Scott promised, closing his hand about hers.

"Oh, Scott—" she said in a frightened whisper. "We're so in the dark."

"I've got to get into the closed wing," Scott said. "We'll have to make sure Obermann is occupied. The school teachers," he decided. "They're three charming old romantics. We'll have to enlist their help in keeping Obermann in the villa for an hour. That'll give me a chance to search around. Tony has to be there!"

"We can't tell them the truth—" Lisa foundered uncertainly. "They'll probably think we're hysterical."

"I have a hunch they'll be willing to go along," Scott guessed. "You don't have to tell them everything, just that it's important to keep Obermann— and Pia and the contessa—in the house for a definite period of time; just hint of some nefarious doings," he smiled indulgently. "Our English schoolteachers harbor vivid imaginations beneath those prim exteriors."

"You want *me* to approach them?" Lisa's eyes fluttered wide. "I think you'd have better luck."

"No," he shook his head firmly. "I would have to be specific. You can get away with being vague. They'll be full of all kinds of romantic notions about the two of us," he teased.

"So?" She lifted an eyebrow in challenge. The look

on Scott's face told her such "notions" definitely filled
his thoughts.

"We'll have time for ourselves later, honey." His
hands reached for one of hers. "After we've cleared
up this mess."

Lisa came down to the drawing room well ahead of
dinner, aware that the English ladies were already
below. She walked into the room with a warm smile.

"Ah, Miss Kirby," Mrs. Eddy welcomed her, patting a corner of the sofa. "How is our young American enjoying her stay?"

"It's all so lovely," Lisa said. She sat down beside
Mrs. Eddy and searched for an approach to enlist
their help.

"You really must see all of Italy," Miss King urged
enthusiastically. "There is no country in Europe quite
like it. Her eyes took on a twinkle. "Our Mr. Anderson, too, should not let this opportunity pass him by.
So far, we've been working on a definite plan. We've
seen Rome, Perugia, Pisa, Sienna, some of the fabulous little villages around them. Did you know?"
Miss King's voice took on a fervent glow of excitement, "that Rome is more than twenty-seven hundred years old?"

"You mustn't miss the Sistine Chapel," Miss Lounsbury took up. "Oh, Miss Kirby, the Michelangelo
frescoes!"

"Yes, I plan on some side tours later in my stay."
Lisa felt herself grow warm. "Mr. Anderson does too."
She took courage from the pleased, knowing looks
the English ladies exchanged.

"Scott is also anxious to see Venice," she said, recalling that the ladies had recently been to Venice.

"Ah, yes," Mrs. Eddy chirped ebulliently. "Venice, the city of romance, wonderful shops along the Ponte Rialto, St. Mark's, the Santa Maria Gloriosa dei Frari with the tomb of Titian, his 'Assumption of the Virgin'. Venice is fabulous."

"You've probably taken millions of photographs?" Lisa pried eagerly, a plan forming in her mind.

"Color slides," Miss Lounsbury corrected with pride. "Althea," she nodded towards Miss King, "has a marvelous sense of proportion—we'll have a collection to be proud of when we return from our sabbatical."

"I'd love to see them," Lisa began persuasively, her air deferential, eager. "Do you have a projector and screen with you?"

"No, it would be too much to carry about," Mrs. Eddy replied. "But perhaps there is such equipment at the villa," she brightened. "With tourists around the place it is just possible."

Pia walked into the drawing room carrying the cocktails that the contessa and she considered peculiarly American but nevertheless condescended to provide. Lisa remembered the brochure mentioned the conversational cocktail hour. Pia served the waiting guests and deposited a tray with shaker and glass, no doubt intended for Scott, on a marble-topped table at a far corner of the room.

"What a handsome young woman," Mrs. Eddy said softly to Lisa as Pia switched on the full battery of her charm for the benefit of the two English ladies. "Amazing that she stays here at the villa. Not that it isn't an exquisite place to live," Mrs. Eddy added quickly. "But Signora Menotti?" She lifted an eyebrow in quizzical disbelief.

"Mrs. Eddy," Lisa said hopefully, her voice subdued, "Scott and I need your help so desperately."

"What can I do?" Mrs. Eddy's eyes were alive to the request. However, she maintained her English calm, in no way betraying that Lisa had asked anything more urgent than the time of day.

"Scott needs time to move about the grounds without being observed," Lisa pursued in an intense whisper, without concerning herself about an explanation. "If somehow we could manage to make sure Mr. Obermann—and the Contessa and Pia—remain here in the drawing room for a while . . . perhaps if you were to show the slides you've collected so far," Lisa ventured breathlessly.

"Sounds practical." Still the cool, undisturbed voice, yet Lisa sensed the eager curiosity her request had aroused. Scott was right, of course, about the English guests. "Why don't I just mention it tonight before dinner? We could show the slides right after dinner," Mrs. Eddy plotted in triumph. "Would that satisfy you?"

"It would be a blessing," Lisa said tremulously, faltering before the older woman's look of sympathy.

"We'll arrange it," Mrs. Eddy promised, patting Lisa's arm.

Scott sauntered into the drawing room and was instantly the center of attention. Pia Menotti walked across to the cocktail shaker and poured Scott a drink. Glass in hand, she moved with a provocative, swinging gait to meet Scott.

"I hope you enjoyed your luncheon in town today," Pia challenged, her eyes holding Scott's.

Lisa watched, aware that the Englishwomen were also watching with quiet disapproval. They had earmarked Scott for Lisa.

"We had a fabulous lunch," Scott said calmly, with quiet emphasis on the "we". "If we had known you had an errand in town, we would have taken care of it for you."

"It was really unimportant," Pia shrugged. "I sometimes fabricate these errands to get away from the villa."

Lisa fumed. How could Pia be so obvious, draping herself about Scott the way she was this minute! Or was this a definite strategy to ferret out Scott's real reason for being in town? Had either Pia or Carl spied Scott phoning at the hotel? Lisa wondered uneasily. No doubt Pia was wondering why Scott had permitted Lisa to go chasing off to the apothecary alone while he waited for luncheon to be served.

"Oh, Senora Menotti," Mrs. Eddy bore down on Pia and Scott, with a tiny secretive glance in Scott's direction. "I was wondering if the villa might have a projector and screen about? I'm so anxious to show you all the slides we've taken so far in our trips about Italy."

"Sounds like fun," Lisa approved. "There's so very much to be seen and six weeks is such a little time."

"Yes," Pia drawled, "we must devise some tours for you, Miss Kirby. But I am so sorry about the screen and slides projector," Pia said in apology and turned to Mrs. Eddy. "I am afraid we have nothing of the sort about the villa."

"I'm sure there must be something like that in the camera shop I saw in town," Scott decided pleasantly, though Lisa detected an air of anxiety. He was aware that Lisa had plotted with Mrs. Eddy as planned.

"I'll run into town tomorrow and see what I can pick up," he promised. "Then we can all have a private showing of the highlights of Italy after dinner tomorrow evening."

"Lovely!" Mrs. Eddy purred, "You American men are so resourceful."

Scott had just included *himself* on the guest list for tomorrow evening, Lisa realized in a panic. Just how was he going to insure Obermann's presence— and his own absence? Another twenty-four hours shot. In a few days Pia Menotti would return to the apothecary to pick up the medication she had ordered with heaven knows what Borgia-like plot in mind?

NINE

Outside the villa, the rain came down in relentless torrents. In her room, Lisa roamed about restlessly. She checked her watch. Almost time to go downstairs for luncheon. For the first time since she had arrived at the villa, luncheon would be served indoors. Scott would surely be back by lunch time, she assured herself. He had taken the ten o'clock bus into town to see about renting the equipment for showing the slides. There had been time for only a few moments' private exchange last night. Pia had seemed to be making a point of keeping Scott and Lisa apart.

Scott was counting on her to keep Carl Obermann a member of their little party, Lisa reminded herself apprehensively. Scott was awfully confident of her capabilities! Carl would be at dinner, or at least join the others for coffee; he was now an accepted member of the household. The three English ladies regarded him with suspicion, Lisa noted. It was the German accent and his clipped military air. After all, the Misses Lounsbury and King and Mrs. Eddy had spent the World War II years in bomb-ridden England. When she had enlisted their aid, they must have immediately conjured up some dramatic explanation, probably tagging Scott as an undercover agent, Lisa guessed, with a flicker of humor.

All right, time to go downstairs for lunch, Lisa decided. She took a swift inventory of herself in the mirror. Last night at dinner Carl Obermann had been surprisingly attentive. He lost his formidable manner in social situations. He was astonishingly well read, she remembered with respect. He was a truly cosmopolitan person, conversant with the arts. Her initial impression had been so wrong, Lisa thought with recurrent astonishment.

As Lisa made her way downstairs, she could hear Mrs. Eddy arguing good-humoredly with a companion in the drawing room. In a rough moment, Scott and she would find allies in the school teachers. What about Rosa, she wondered, seeing her heavy, immaculately uniformed body moving towards the small dining room. Maybe Scott could get through to Rosa.

A motor scooter pulled to a stop outside in the driveway, and instinctively Lisa made a move towards the door. Maria sprinted past her. A delivery boy, Lisa learned. She walked toward the drawing room slowly so that she might hear the repartee between Maria and the young man with a package.

"Grazie, grazie," Maria wound up reluctantly, and hurried towards the rear of the house again with the water-spattered package.

The delivery boy had come from the camera shop in town. Where was Scott, Lisa wondered with rising apprehension? Why had he sent these things out instead of bringing them with him? Or had the villa arranged for the equipment? No, Scott had made a point of offering to go into the village; had there been some switch in plan since last night? She had spoken to him for only a split-second on the balcony when he was breakfasting. He said he was racing to make the ten o'clock bus. Then where was he, she asked herself again, pushing down panic.

"The rains have finally caught up with us," Mrs. Eddy greeted her effervescently. The contessa, in her inevitable severely cut black frock with its air of Paris high fashion, had been dutifully playing the hostess; she now retreated with obvious relief.

"You will excuse me," the contessa tossed over one shoulder. "I will see what is being done about luncheon."

"Where is your Mr. Anderson this morning?" Mrs. Eddy whispered, her eyes bright.

"He went into town to see about the equipment. I gather it just arrived." Not really *her* Mr. Anderson, Lisa thought nervously.

"Oh, is he staying in town for luncheon?"

It was impossible to resent the show of interest, Lisa admitted; there was such friendliness behind Mrs. Eddy's curiosity.

"I don't know if he's coming back in time for lunch," Lisa reported candidly. "I only had a moment to talk to him this morning." She hoped uneasily that the school teacher wouldn't probe about the reasons for enlisting their aid. What on earth could she say?

"Signora Menotti went into town this morning also," Mrs. Eddy went on, with a confiding air. Lisa looked up sharply. "I know because I saw the Mercedes headed down the driveway. Was Mr. Anderson able to get a lift into town with her?"

"What time was that?" Lisa asked, trying not to show that she was surprised.

"Oh, about twenty past ten."

"He was taking the ten o'clock bus," Lisa said, wishing that the other English ladies would join them and end this conversation that could become uncomfortable any moment. Had Pia followed Scott into town? Where were the two of them now? Scott hadn't planned to meet Pia in town, had he? Warmth colored her cheeks as she considered this.

"How does Mr. Anderson anticipate making sure that Signor Obermann stays here in the house?" Mrs. Eddy whispered, and Lisa realized that she was enjoying the situation enormously.

"He's counting on us to make sure of that," Lisa confessed, grateful for the chance to enlist the other's assistance.

"Then we'll just have to do it," Mrs. Eddy said firmly. "Perhaps he's going to stay on in town all day to make it easier for himself," Mrs. Eddy deduced.

"That's quite possible," Lisa acknowledged.

Something akin to relief welled in her. Why hadn't she realized that, Lisa thought. No need to worry about Scott's absence; it was no doubt plotted. Yet she couldn't feel entirely at ease when Pia Menotti was also missing from the villa.

The two English spinsters joined Lisa and Mrs. Eddy, chatting wistfully about the rain. Only now did Lisa discover that they had planned to leave this morning for a trip to Torre del Lego, where Puccini had lived. Miss King, in her youth, had nurtured dreams of an operatic career. The trip was postponed in favor of assisting Lisa and Scott.

"Rosa is serving luncheon in the smaller dining salon," the contessa announced from the doorway. She smiled the supercilious smile that never failed to arouse Lisa's smoldering anger. She had probably not been so supercilious to her Fascist lovers.

The four guests obediently headed for the luncheon table to find Maria setting forth savory plates of gnocchi. A salad bowl already waited on the table along with a linen-covered platter of hot rolls. The contessa poured wine into delicately fashioned goblets with the air of royalty presiding at a state banquet.

"Contessa," Mrs. Eddy began eagerly. "Only this morning I noticed the small painting above the console table in the foyer—"

"A copy," the contessa interrupted, a look on her face that said she had heard this question many times before. "Like many of the paintings you see about the villa. During the war our villa was pillaged, first by the Fascists, then the Nazis. Priceless treasures, in the family for generations were spirited away. Someday," the faded blue eyes took on an odd glitter, "someday the villa may be restored to its former magnificence."

"But after the war?" Miss King's high-pitched voice pursued. "Weren't you able to reclaim what was taken? The paintings, jewelry?" Lisa realized that the Englishwomen had heard the stories of the villa's being stripped of its treasures before. "Were you not able to demand restitution by the government?"

The contessa shrugged with a hint of annoyance. "We tried to deal with the government. Both our own, and the German government. It was useless." Lisa began putting together a few fragments of information. Excitement caught hold of her as the picture formed in her mind. The priceless paintings, the jewelry, about which the contessa was now talking with impassioned anger, had not been spirited away by the Fascists! They would have been reclaimed at the end of the war. Those treasures lay hidden somewhere about the Villa Como! Pia knew this and so did the contessa. And Lisa's mother! Was this what her mother had referred to as belonging to *her?*

Lisa sat at the table, a polite smile on her mouth, her mind racing ahead. Why didn't Scott come back? She couldn't wait to offer this new theory. In some way Tony must be a block to the contessa's finding the cache, Lisa thought. Surely the contessa knew every corner of the villa by now. How could something like that be concealed without her being able to make the discovery? Was that why Obermann was here, too, to help in the search? What about Tony? How did her brother fit into this strange mosaic? Did he know and refuse to talk? Were they trying to force his hand? Oddly, this possibility was a relief. They couldn't afford to annihilate Tony Menotti if he were the only living link to the secret of the Villa Como—not before he revealed that secret!

Luncheon was over, and the contessa withdrew without delay. A slight chill had settled about the villa with its enormous high-ceilinged rooms. Maria came into the drawing room to start the fire. The pungent aroma of the olive branches began to circulate about the room.

"What a beautiful way to spend a rainy day," Miss Lounsbury murmured sentimentally, relaxing in a chair beside the gigantic marble-faced fireplace.

"There hasn't been much rain since I arrived," Lisa said. "I can't really complain." She should go on upstairs to her room, Lisa cautioned herself, before the women began to probe. The curiosity was there behind all their eyes.

"It's been amazingly fine since our arrival in Italy," Miss King said. "And that's been almost seven weeks."

"There was just one bad spell," Mrs. Eddy recalled, and something in her voice compelled Lisa's attention. "It rained for three days, almost without let-up." Her voice dropped to exclude anyone not within their immediate circle. "That was the time Signora Menotti arrived here at the villa. It was in the middle of the night, in the company of two men." Mrs. Eddy's eyes watched Lisa with friendly candor. "I was awake because I was having trouble with my sinus condition at the time and found it impossible to sleep. The black Mercedes drove up in front of the villa—I can see the entrance from my room. Two men got out with her. It was raining heavily and it was dark outside—I couldn't see who it was, of course, except one was a woman and the other two, men."

"That's right," Miss Lounsbury picked up avidly. "Next day, Pia walked in when we were having lunch—you know that way she has—" A twinkle showed itself in Miss Lounsbury's eyes. "As though she's constantly afraid one of us might infect her with germs? Though I notice that only applies to the female sex. Men are entirely harmless," she finished.

"Don't be catty, Caroline," Mrs. Eddy admonished.

"That was the first we heard of the contessa's daughter-in-law. The contessa herself had answered our inquiries about accommodations. I wonder," Miss King said thoughtfully, "if Signor Obermann was one of those men that arrived during the storm? And who was the other man?"

"When did she arrive?" Lisa asked urgently.

"About six weeks ago," Mrs. Eddy began.

Mrs. Eddy's voice trailed off; she stiffened, her face suddenly rosy. Lisa followed her gaze. Pia Menotti was walking towards them with panther-like quietness. Lisa's eyes swung back to Mrs. Eddy, reassuring her they could not have been overheard. But it was difficult to mask her own excitement as Lisa began to add up the latest fragments of information. Pia had arrived in the middle of the night with Carl Obermann—and Tony! Just at the time Tony disappeared from Paris.

Lisa moved slowly about her room as she dressed

for dinner. Before going up to her room, she had asked that towels be sent up, in a fervent hope that the bearer would be Rosa. Time was growing too short—she would take a chance on questioning Rosa, hoping for an ally.

She walked to the balcony for the dozenth time in the last hour, listening for sounds in the next room. Scott had not yet returned. There was a light knock on the door, and Lisa hurried to open it.

"Tovaglia," Rosa offered hesitantly, walking into the room.

"Grazie," Lisa smiled. "I'm afraid I use so many. *Multo,"* she pretended to be searching for the word. "Rosa," she said, suddenly desperate as Rosa turned to leave.

"Si Signorina?" The dark eyes watchful.

"Has Mr. Anderson returned yet?" she asked retreating.

"I no see," Rosa shrugged.

"Rosa—" she hesitated, ordering herself to gamble. "Where is Tony?" Rosa paled with shock. "Is he here at the villa, Rosa?" Her eyes searched Rosa's, pleading.

"No comprendo," Rosa gasped.

"Is Tony here in the villa?" Lisa repeated in Italian. "Rosa, is he all right?"

"You go!" Rosa whispered, unnerved that Lisa spoke Italian. "The contessa warned you come to make trouble!"

"Why?" Lisa probed. "Why did the contessa think I came to make trouble?"

"The Signora," Rosa said, the words halting. "She think because you are artist, you know too much.

Leave the villa, Signorina Kirby. Much trouble if you stay!" All at once she waddled from the room in a burst of speed, slamming the door behind her.

Rosa had not denied that Tony was here. Rosa knew now that Lisa spoke Italian, believed that she *knew* Tony and understood that the role of a young American tourist was no more than a cover. But no one could guess who Lisa Kirby really was.

Would Rosa confide her discovery to the contessa, Lisa wondered in alarm? Perhaps Rosa had warned her to leave earlier just in hope of avoiding trouble for the Menottis. Whose side was Rosa on? Lisa's own life might depend on the answer to that.

Lisa sat down, fumbled for a cigarette, not that she particularly cared about smoking but the action steadied her. Scott would be upset that she had given herself away to Rosa. That stupid, impulsive streak of hers again!

No time to worry about that now, Lisa reminded herself. After dinner Mrs. Eddy and her friends would show their slides. Somehow, the contessa, Pia and Signor Obermann had to be kept within the villa. Obermann sometimes sat down to dinner with them, sometimes only appeared for coffee. Scott knew that they usually finished dinner at the same time— he was counting on at least forty minutes after dinner.

The Englishwomen were chattering with Pia and the contessa when Lisa joined them downstairs. Was it her imagination, Lisa wondered nervously, or were the contessa and Pia unusually excited this evening?

"Signor Anderson phoned," the contessa reported

as the six women walked towards the dining salon.
"He found it necessary to drive into Milan for a replacement part for his typewriter. We are not to expect him for dinner."

Dear God, let Obermann show up, Lisa thought in
panic. That was all Scott needed, after the phone call
about Milan—to walk into Carl Obermann around
the grounds tonight. Thank heavens the heavy downpour of the morning had subsided. A full moon now
poured a silver brightness about the villa.

"Surely Signor Obermann will join us later?" Miss
King pursued with a coy smile. "We certainly need a
man to help us with the equipment. Women are always so helpless in the face of mechanical things."

"He will join us for coffee," the contessa said after
a moment, and later Lisa heard her instructing Rosa,
in Italian, to order him to the drawing room. Rosa's
eyes swung involuntarily to Lisa's for an instant because Rosa knew—as the contessa obviously did not
—that Lisa Kirby understood Italian as well as anybody in the villa. Rosa had not confided in the contessa.

Lisa was filled with relief when Carl Obermann appeared in the drawing room as coffee was being
served. He gravitated towards Lisa; she sensed it was
with deliberate intent. Tonight Pia made a point of
ignoring Carl.

"We're seeing the slides tonight," Lisa forced herself into a show of conviviality. "I understand you've
been elected to the job of projectionist."

"I shall try," Carl shrugged. "I am honored by your
trust." There was good-humored mockery in his
smile.

Lisa settled herself in a chair, her mind beset with anxieties about Scott; he must be searching about the closed wing of the villa at that very moment. Had they been rash in assuming no one else was on guard in Carl's absence? Scott wasn't even armed! Or was he? The possibility that Scott, too, might be armed increased her tension.

Lisa tried to take part in the sprightly conversation elicited by each new color slide that flashed on the screen. If she weren't so upset, Lisa admitted, she would have been impressed. She kept sneaking looks at her watch in the darkened room, reading the hands in the spill of moonlight. An hour could pass so quickly! Where was Scott? Had he discovered Tony? Was Scott all right?

The lights were turned on; Mrs. Eddy and Carl busily put away the equipment and slides. With a touch of panic Lisa noted that the contessa had slipped from the room in the darkness. Where was she? From the guarded looks being exchanged by the Englishwomen, Lisa knew they, too, were conscious of the contessa's absence.

As though by prearrangement, first Carl, then Pia withdrew for the evening. The others were deeply concerned that Scott had not yet returned to the villa.

"It's been a long day inside the villa, what with all the rain," Mrs. Eddy said trying to be cheerful. "I suggest we all retire early."

"I'm drowsy already," Miss King conceded. "And there's so much to do in these next few days. You know, we're leaving on Friday, my dear," she confided to Lisa.

"No, I didn't know!" Lisa's eyes widened. She wished they were staying on at the villa.

"We've decided to fly straight to Naples," Mrs. Eddy said. "We'll miss the villa—it's been such a marvelous experience."

Lisa lay in bed on her side, eyes fastened to the door. Where was Scott? Why didn't he come back to the villa? It was late; he should be back by now. Didn't he know she was going out of her mind with worry? Had something happened to him? If Scott were not in his room by breakfast time, Lisa resolved to go straight to the police!

Despite her concern for Scott, Lisa eventually found her eyelids drooping with tiredness. Against her will, she slept. And then, Lisa lay stiff with fear, fully awake. Again, an intruder in her dressing room! In the stillness, she could hear the labored breathing of someone moving under stress.

Her hands trembled as she noiselessly moved back the covers and started in bare feet for the door. A figure emerging from the dressing room. It was a woman. Lisa tried to scream. Something soft came down over her face, cutting off her breath. Blackness enveloped her. . . .

Slowly, Lisa returned to consciousness, aware of voices in the room.

"Not yet, Rosa," Lisa heard Scott exhort. "Wait until she's fully conscious."

Lisa's eyes opened, showing her relief at finding Scott with her. Rosa was hovering over her with a cup of steaming coffee.

"Oh, Scott," Lisa whispered, shivering.

"Take it easy, baby," Scott coaxed. "You're all right."

"It was a woman," Lisa managed. "In my dressing room. I tried to make it to the door. I couldn't see who it was—only the figure of a woman."

"She must have come at you with a pillow," Scott said tightly. "We found it on the floor beside you. I must have frightened her away."

"Oh, Scott, if you hadn't been here!" She shuddered.

"Easy, baby," he soothed, his eyes anxious.

"What about the others?" Lisa asked, trying to clear her head.

"Nobody heard you except me. I was just coming up to my room. I heard you—tried the door. It was open."

"I locked it," Lisa whispered. "I'm sure I locked it."

"The windows and balcony door were locked," Scott said seriously. "There's a panel behind the tapestry in your dressing room that leads into my dressing room."

Lisa's mouth gaped in amazement. "You found that out just now?"

"The tapestry was pushed aside," Scott explained. "Whoever she was, she escaped through my room— while I was in here with you."

"But nobody will believe me, will they?" Lisa challenged. "It'll be another nightmare."

"We'll see," Scott said tensely.

"*Caffe?*" Rosa enticed gently.

"Rosa was still in the kitchen; I brought her up to

help," Scott said. "I thought it might be necessary to phone for a doctor."

"No, I'm all right," Lisa whispered huskily, turning questioningly to Rosa. What was Rosa doing in the kitchen in the middle of the night? What had Scott found out?

"Caffe?" Rosa coaxed worriedly again.

"I'll never go back to sleep after coffee at this hour," Lisa improvised. She must talk to Scott alone!

"Tea," Scott ordered. "Would you mind, Rosa?"

"Subito," Rosa promised, and trundled off.

Lisa waited until the door was firmly closed and they could hear Rosa descending the stair.

"Scott, what did you find out?"

"I got clobbered over the head before I could get over the villa wall," Scott said grimly.

"Oh, Scott!" Lisa's eyes darkened in compassion. Only now did she notice the bruise across his forehead. "The contessa walked out in the midst of the slides tonight," she remembered, squinting in thought.

"It wasn't the contessa," Scott reassured her with a touch of humor. "I had got off the bus, and was walking towards the gate, figuring on scaling the wall near the house to save time." His voice was discreetly low. "Wham, something came at me! I could swear," Scott said curiously, "that it was our friend the waiter again."

"Then we'll go to the police," Lisa said quickly. "We can't go on this way!"

"Not yet," Scott demurred, an eye on the door for Rosa's return.

"Scott, the Englishwomen told me Pia arrived

about six weeks ago, in the middle of the night—with two men."

"Obermann and Tony," Scott concluded. "Lisa, you didn't spill anything to the old girls?" he asked anxiously.

"Nothing," Lisa said quickly. "But I spoke to Rosa," she conceded unhappily. "I asked her about Tony."

"Oh, Lord!" Scott was shocked. And then suspicion crept into his voice. "Your locket? Is it where you left it when you went to bed?"

"I have it right here," Lisa said, pulling the gold chain from beneath the neckline of her pajamas. "Scott, do you think she was after the locket?"

"Where do you usually keep it?" Scott was on his feet.

"Locked in the small jewelry box on the dressing table inside," Lisa told him, and watched as he wheeled about and headed for the dressing room.

In a few moments Scott returned with the attractive little jewelry box that had been her mother's. The lock had been broken open.

"Oh, Scott," Lisa whispered, stunned. "Only Rosa could have known I usually keep it there!"

TEN

Rosa returned with a tray of tea, poured two cups, and left them alone, pointedly leaving the door ajar.

"She's concerned for your honor," Scott grinned.

"I'm concerned about other things," Lisa said grimly, then smiled faintly at the laughter in Scott's eyes. "Scott, I never suspected that sweet old woman—"

"Don't pin it on Rose," Scott objected. "Any woman searching in your room would automatically have thought of trying the jewelry box."

"Scott, who could it have been?" Certainly it was none of the Englishwomen. That left Maria, the contessa or Pia. "It couldn't have been Rosa," Lisa realized with relief. "The woman wasn't heavy like Rosa."

"We can't pin it down to anybody," Scott reminded her gently. "You didn't actually see the woman."

"Nothing is missing from the box," Lisa said, checking the contents. She sighed and touched the broken lock. "Do you suppose this can be fixed? It was my mother's." A flood of memory brought tears to her eyes.

"I'll take it into town and have it repaired. Good as new," Scott promised.

"Mrs. Eddy and her friends are leaving Friday," Lisa began.

"I want you to go with them," Scott said firmly.

"No," Lisa refused. "So you can wander around getting your head banged up? Scott, you might have been killed." She shuddered, almost spilling the hot tea.

"I don't want you here, honey, in this kind of danger."

"I won't go, Scott," Lisa insisted. "Not without you. I can't leave when I'm so sure Tony is here. I keep remembering the drugs Pia is scheduled to pick up."

His eyes narrowed thoughtfully. "I must have my source of information check further on Obermann to see if he has some medical background."

"What could that mean?" Lisa sought for a link between Carl Obermann's possible medical background and the drugs Pia Menotti had ordered from Milan.

"I don't know," Scott admitted. "I'm just fishing. I don't know what it might add up to."

"What are you telling the others about tonight?" Lisa asked after a moment.

"Absolutely nothing." He startled her with his firmness. "I told Rosa, too, to forget it." He smiled faintly. "She seemed quite willing."

"But how can we?" Lisa protested.

"Because time is short," Scott said. "I don't want to get involved with more play-acting with the contessa and Pia." He squinted in thought. "I don't like to get you involved more deeply than you already are—"

"What do you want me to do?" Lisa demanded quickly. "Scott, I *am* involved!"

"I notice that you and Obermann are on a friendly basis." For an instant a gentle amusement showed in his eyes. "I have to have time to give that left wing a going-over. Rotten luck to get loused up the way I did."

"Why do you think the waiter went after you like that?" Lisa asked. There was no doubt in her mind that it had been the waiter.

"Possibly he didn't want me to see him going into the villa," Scott guessed. "He may be making some deal with the contessa."

"Scott, I forgot to tell you!" Lisa started guiltily. "At lunch today the contessa was talking about the treasures the Fascists and Nazis confiscated from the villa. When Mrs. Eddy—or one of the others— asked about reclaiming their possessions after the war, the contessa was annoyed. Scott, do you suppose the paintings and the jewelry could be hidden here at the Villa?"

"You're jumping to conclusions again," he warned.

"It could be," she insisted.

"Let's get back to tomorrow night," Scott said. "Getting Obermann out of the way. There just isn't enough time during that short period when he comes in to have his coffee after dinner—"

"If there could be some way of making sure he is at dinner," Lisa said slowly, and colored because she knew Scott was reading her mind. If she flirted with Obermann, coaxed him into the house for dinner—but that was too nebulous. They had no time for vague possibilities.

"What about discovering you've lost your locket while you're having coffee," Scott plotted. "Ask Obermann to go out with you to search around the area where you've been painting. That's situated so that I could skirt around towards the back of the house without being seen. Keep him occupied as long as you can, then make sure he walks you back to the villa."

"Will that be long enough?" Lisa asked with anxiety.

"It'll have to be."

"Scott, be careful," Lisa pleaded.

"I'd better get out of here," Scott said reluctantly. "Before Rosa comes up and throws me out."

Lisa realized that Scott was making a point of staying in his room. He typed steadily all morning, not even appearing downstairs for luncheon. Lisa spied Maria, tray in hand, heading for Scott's room. Also he needed to wait for the swelling on his forehead to subside.

There was no indication among the others that anything unusual might have happened the night before. If the contessa or Pia knew anything of Scott's misadventure, they concealed it completely. Only Rosa, in brief appearances, looked apprehensive.

Tony was here! Her brother, whom she had never seen and who was now her whole family. Scott was sure Tony was here. There was a quiet desperation about Scott that made her uneasy for his safety. And she was uncomfortable, too, before the mounting curiosity of the three school teachers.

"You look tired, Miss Kirby," Mrs. Eddy observed solicitously. Rosa moved about the terrace luncheon table with tall glasses of iced coffee.

"It's so hot," Lisa tried to sound natural. "On days like this I should cut down my morning painting schedule."

"It must be such a wonderful feeling," Miss King observed wistfully, "to be able to satisfy your creative instincts."

"The problem is to satisfy yourself," Lisa laughed. "Nothing ever seems quite good enough."

"Every artist considers himself a perfectionist," Pia

commented. "It must make life a bore sometimes."

"I'm never bored," Lisa retaliated.

Was it Pia in her room last night? It could have been. What had the waiter told the contessa last night, when he crept into the villa? He was probably a relative of Maria's, Lisa guessed. No doubt, the contessa had been expecting him.

"Are we going to see some of your canvases?" Mrs. Eddy asked. "We're leaving Friday, you know."

"I have nothing finished," Lisa confessed.

Lisa tried to concentrate on the table conversation. She was beginning to understand the furtive, curious glances the English ladies were sending in her direc-rection. They were wondering about last night. They couldn't know the whole plot had fizzled.

"I'm sorry we decided again't Torro del Lago yes-terday," Miss King said wistfully. "It was where Puccini lived."

"It was raining like fury yesterday," Miss Louns-bury reminded her. "It would have been too dreary."

"Who will be taking our places, Signora Menotti?" Mrs. Eddy asked Pia. "More of our countrymen?"

"There were two English couples, one with a child," Pia said. "At the last moment they had found it neces-sary to cancel." Pia's look defied anyone to probe more deeply.

"Will you all excuse me?" Lisa said softly. "I think I'll settle in for a long siesta."

Lisa walked quickly up the stairs to her room, not wanting to think of the villa shorn of guests except for Scott and herself. There was no sound of typing from Scott's room now. His tray waited on the floor just outside his door. Lisa let herself into her room, closed the door, slowly walked across the room. Stretching out on the bed, she stared up at the ceiling and thought about tonight's project.

It was dangerous for Scott to go prowling around that way. Timing was critical. She would have to keep Carl lingering over coffee. She would have to inveigle him into helping her search for the locket. She would have to drag out every possible moment while they searched the grounds.

Lisa sat up. She heard a low regular tapping coming from inside her dressing room. She darted across the bedroom into the dressing room. Her hands eagerly reached for the tapestry that masked the hidden panel. Even as she searched for some spring that would move the panel it slid open.

"Hi," Scott grinned. He had to stoop to look at her because he was inches too tall for the opening. "Am I invited inside?"

"Of course," she said breathlessly. "Though I'm sure Rosa would never approve."

Scott lowered his head and ducked through the opening. "I've been keeping to my room in case anybody got curious about this." He indicated the bruise above his left eye. "I wouldn't want our English friends to get overly solicitous and drag in the police."

"What about the contessa?" Lisa asked. "Isn't she curious about why you're staying up here?"

"I told Maria that I was knee-deep in work—on a streak where the stuff is just pouring out. I'll have dinner upstairs, too."

"How will you get out?" she asked worriedly, walking with Scott into the other room. He put his arm about her waist. "Scott, it's so dangerous. If they find out—" her voice broke off.

"I'll get out by way of the balcony," Scott said calmly. "It isn't too much of a drop for a man in good physical shape." He chuckled. "Not that I'm bragging."

"Suppose Carl doesn't go along?" Lisa prodded. "Scott, we don't know what he'll do!"

"I have a fair idea," Scott said grimly. "But don't worry. Obermann will go along."

"How do you know?"

"Because he's a man, and you're a very luscious young dish," Scott said calmly. "And that's all the compliments you'll get out of me today. What time did the post arrive, did you happen to notice?" He reached into his jacket pocket.

"About half-past eleven. It was a little late—I heard Miss King mention it. Why?"

"I wanted to make sure this hadn't been tampered with," Scott explained, pulling a letter out of an envelope. "I don't think so—Maria brought it up well before noon."

"What is it?"

"From my friend in Paris. He did some more research on his own. The letter is carefully worded—discusses a plot for a novel—but they might pick up the drift. The substance of the letter is this: Carl Obermann stopped medical school six months short of graduation, to serve the Fuhrer at Buchenwald. He won high commendation for his experiments with brain-washing drugs, drugs that could produce insanity—"

"Oh, no!" Lisa gasped with horror. "The drugs Pia ordered in town. Scott, are they planning to drive Tony insane?"

"That would be one way to secure control of the villa," he said. "To have Tony committed."

"With this information about Carl Obermann, why can't we go to the police?" Lisa urged. "It makes sense now, doesn't it?"

"Carl Obermann served seventeen months in prison for his war crimes," Scott said. "And then Herr Obermann was released—for good behavior."

"How will I ever go through with tonight's plan?" Lisa whispered. "Knowing about him!"

"Maybe I shouldn't have told you," Scott berated himself. "It's more important than ever now that I get into the closed wing. Stall him, honey. Stall him, for every precious moment you can wangle. I don't think he'll give you too rough a time—"

Carl Obermann wouldn't make a play for her, not practically beneath Pia's nose. "He's being the perfect gentleman right now," Lisa said somberly. "He's working too hard at that impression to make a false move."

"I'd better get back into my room. We'll time everything to the minute tonight. I'll be able to hear Carl come into the house and head out by way of the balcony. The dining salon is on the far side—they can't possibly hear me."

"I'll try to keep him occupied as long as I can," Lisa promised. "But do you know, nobody let on at all about last night! I just thought they might—"

"Not this crew," Scott rejected. "They're tough

and unscrupulous. Anything goes." His hand reached
for hers, pressed it tightly. "Lisa, be careful. We're in
this together now—the three of us. Tony, you and I!"

ELEVEN

Lisa found that she was trembling as she finished dressing for dinner. She deliberately wore a simple black
crepe blouse over a matching skirt, and a rope of
pearls that lent her an air of sophistication beyond her
years. Her mother had teased her for buying black
because she normally loved dramatic colors and off-
beat combinations.

Her locket was conspicuously missing; its heavy
gold chain lay demurely beneath the pearls. Lisa had
sewn the locket into her brassiere, where the fullness
of her blouse would conceal its small bulge. It would
seem that she wore the locket beneath the pearls.
Then, when she pulled forth the chain and pretended
shock at the absence of the locket, the situation would
ring true.

Lisa took care with her makeup—mascara tonight
for the already curling dark lashes, an irridescent turquoise eyeshadow to highlight the loveliness of her
eyes. Delicate touches of lipstick emphasized the
creaminess of her skin. The black dramatized her
slender figure, giving her an air of fragility.

Lisa waited until the last moment to go downstairs
for dinner. She was anxious to avoid conversation
with the others tonight.

Maria was peering up the stairway. "The contessa say you come please to dinner." Maria's eyes swept over Lisa with a look that told Lisa the extra effort tonight had been worth while.

"I'm sorry to be late." Lisa smiled perfunctorily. She wasn't actually late. Dinner was not scheduled to be served for another five minutes. But the contessa was accustomed to the guests gathering together earlier.

Lisa walked straight into the dining salon. The others were drifting in from the opposite entrance. Lisa spied Carl in conversation with Pia. So Carl was going to be here for dinner tonight! She hesitated, debating about returning upstairs to alert Scott that Carl was at the table. That extra time would be useful! No, a little thing like that might be a giveaway to the others, Lisa cautioned herself.

Carl's eyes moved in her direction with a look of admiration that Pia intercepted. Pia said something under her breath. From the look on Pia's face, Lisa guessed it was a scornful remark. But tonight, quite obviously, Carl Obermann found Lisa's fragile loveliness more entrancing than the sultry earthiness of Pia Menotti. He kept looking at Lisa, even while he carried on polite conversation with Pia and Mrs. Eddy.

Dinner began with *Zuppa di Celege al Vino*— cold wine soup with cherries—that brought forth exclamations of delight from the English ladies, and compliments for Rosa from Carl. Tonight Lisa ate without tasting, though she managed a casual show of interest in the dinner. The soup was followed by veal cutlets a la Milanese, brussel sprouts with chestnuts, pickled string beans and an artichoke salad served on a nest of endive.

Would dinner never end, Lisa wondered restlessly, trying to concentrate on the questions being shot at her at regular intervals by the contessa. It was apparent that Lisa was the subject of uneasy suspicions on the part of the two Italian ladies and their German cohort.

What had suddenly triggered the interest in her? The search in her room last night—the waiter's secret entry into the villa—all tied up somehow with the locket! The waiter knew something about the locket that was an impenetrable secret to the rest of them. Somehow it was entangled with Tony's disappearance and the lost treasures of the Villa Como.

Lisa sighed with relief when the group adjourned to the drawing room for after-dinner coffee. She was nervous lest someone remark about her wearing pearls tonight because that would force her hand about the disappearance of her locket. Not yet, she prayed silently. Scott must be provided with enough time to complete his expedition.

Carl made a point of sitting beside her on the ivory brocade sofa as the contessa poured coffee for them.

"I cannot keep my eyes off you tonight, Miss Kirby," Carl murmured softly. "I have never seen you this way."

"What way?" she laughed, head tilted to one angle, flirting lightly.

"You have the look about you tonight of the highborn northern Italian. The blue eyes, the fair skin, the delicate features. Most appealing."

"Thank you," Lisa said softly. She *was* Italian,

Lisa realized. High-born Italian—wouldn't that amuse her friends back home at the Art Students' League?

"You make the pearls beautiful." His eyes glinted with soaring interest. "Lisa," he said, his German accent giving it a harshness. "That could be an Italian name."

"The pearls are synthetic," she said frankly. She looked at the contessa, who also wore pearls. Her heart hammered. Here was an opening for her to discover her locket was missing.

Carl's gaze followed Lisa's to the contessa's multiple strands of pearls. "Also, what you call synthetic. The Menotti jewels belong with the past."

Lisa's fingers crept, trembling slightly, toward her throat.

"I was becoming self-conscious about wearing my locket all the time," Lisa said, aware that the contessa—despite her seeming absorption in conversation with Miss Lounsbury—was beamed in to their conversation. Was it her imagination or did the contessa stiffen at the mention of the locket? "I disguised it with the pearls." Lisa's fingers were at the pearls, thrusting them aside to find the heavy gold chain. "See?" Lisa said pertly, and pulled the chain from beneath the pearls. She wasn't wrong; the contessa's eyes were fastened on the chain. "Oh, no!" Lisa gasped. "It's gone!" She stared at the chain in disbelief.

From the corner of her eye, she saw the contessa swing about in wordless accusation. It had been Pia last night in her room searching for the locket! And now the contessa thought that Pia had stolen it and denied having done so! "How could I have lost it?" Lisa's distress was admirably sincere.

"When was the last time you saw it?" Carl asked calmly. "Think, Lisa." He, too, was conscious of the tense communication between Pia and the contessa.

"When I put it on this morning after I had show-ered and dressed. I wore the locket while I was painting this morning—that was when I slipped it inside my blouse. I had a feeling that it was silly to keep wearing the one thing all the time, but it was my mother's—I'm deeply sentimental about it."

"In the garden, you say?" Carl frowned in thought. Pia glared back at her mother-in-law in triumph because Lisa had just vindicated her.

"Could we go search for it now?" Lisa implored. "I know it's an imposition—"

"We will search straight off," Carl purred. "First let me ask Rosa for a torchlight." He rose swiftly and headed toward the rear of the villa.

"Don't worry, my dear," Mrs. Eddy soothed, yet Lisa was aware of Mrs. Eddy's suspicions that this was just one more angle in the plot not yet revealed to them. "I'm sure you'll find your locket."

"I know it's silly to be so upset over something of so little value," Lisa apologized. "But it's the one piece of jewelry that belonged to my mother that I have."

Lisa felt the intrigue that bristled between the two Italian women. She had claimed that the locket was lying out there in the garden somewhere. But they were apprehensive that someone else—an unknown person—had stolen it. Was she courting danger, go-ing out into the garden that way with Carl? But the locket wouldn't be found, she comforted herself. Carl had no way of knowing she had the locket concealed on herself. He wouldn't try to force the truth from her. Not with the English ladies well aware of the fact that she would be alone in the garden with him.

"All right, Lisa," Carl called to her from the drawing room. "We'll go search."

As Lisa rose from the sofa, she met Pia's eyes for a fleeting instant. Pia was furious with her. For being attractive to Carl? Because Carl called her "Lisa", when he had been so formal up until tonight? Lisa smiled politely to the others and strode quickly toward Carl.

They walked together out into the night, Carl's hand at her elbow, the torchlight illuminating their path. She was conscious of the heaviness of his breathing. The pressure of his hand at her elbow was more than solicitous.

"I usually work down there to the right," she said nervously. "I must have dropped it there."

"It will be difficult to find at night," Carl warned. "Even with the flashlight."

"Please, we must search carefully," Lisa coaxed. She must keep Carl occupied for at least fifteen minutes. That would insure Scott forty minutes of uninterrupted time.

"We will try," Carl promised, his fingers stroking her bare arm as they walked towards her painting cove. "For you, Lisa, anything you ask," he said in an impassioned whisper that alarmed her. Oh, no, not Carl panting on her neck!

"It should be somewhere around here," she indicated nervously as they approached the cypress-hedged enclosure that she had adopted as her own.

From high above the lake, the summer moon bathed the garden in pale light illuminating their faces. He was going to make a play, she thought frantically.

"Tomorrow we will find the locket," Carl promised huskily, his hands caressing her shoulders. "Tomorrow, Lisa."

"But we should look now," Lisa stammered. She had to stall Carl, she reminded herself; she mustn't let him go off into the dark alone, to stumble upon Scott!

"I know what you think of me," he sighed. "This absurd bit about my being a guard for the villa—"

"Isn't it true?" Lisa asked, playing the wide-eyed young American. "That's what the contessa said."

"I am here because of Pia," he said candidly. "She asked me to come. For the contessa's benefit we pretend that I am the villa guard—because of all the trespassers in the neighborhood of late."

"I knew you weren't a guard," Lisa said with an impulsive switch of tactics, and noted the pleased look this elicited.

"How did you know?" His arm folded about her.

"The way you talk, the things you say—you're too well read, too sensitive." She put down a feeling of revulsion that threatened to make this play-acting impossible. She *had* thought Carl Obermann an interesting man just three days ago.

"Why are you pushing me off?" he reproached gently, believing this was a conquest delayed only by a sudden shyness.

"The others inside," Lisa whispered. "Pia . . ."

"To the devil with Pia," he said brusquely. "It was a thing of the moment. I met her in Paris a few months ago—we have some small business to settle now, little else."

Carl's strong hands caressed her back while his mouth slowly moved towards hers.

"Carl, not here," she rejected, swerving her head so that his mouth grazed her throat. She felt sick inside at his touch. "Not here," she said again, fearful of antagonizing him but unable to accept his attentions.

"Where?" His voice was warm with anticipation. "Where, little one?"

"Away from the villa," she stalled, her heart pounding. Just hold him off! "Can we meet somewhere Friday?" she asked, in a panic to delay him.

"Friday in the late afternoon I must drive into town on an errand," he said, his eyebrows furrowed in thought. "You can contrive some errand. I will arrange to drop you off. A duty to a guest," he chuckled. "We will be careful," he promised. "No one will know."

"Meanwhile," Lisa said firmly, "let's look for the locket."

"We will not find it in this darkness, even with the moonlight and the torch," he warned. Lisa sensed he was pleased with himself.

"Carl," Pia's voice intruded. "Maria found this. I thought perhaps it might be more useful."

Lisa and Carl swung about to face Pia. She was standing with a mocking smile on her face, a huge army-type searchlight in hand. Pia and the contessa didn't fully trust Carl, Lisa guessed. They were afraid Carl might find the locket himself, make some secret deal with her!

"Thank you," Carl said with an ironic smile. "Perhaps you would like to stay and help us search?"

Lisa dragged out the hunt for every additional instant she dared. Finally, she agreed with Pia and Carl that it was futile to continue at night. Carl promised to help her again in the morning. The three of them walked back to the house, heading off in separate directions as they arrived in the entrance foyer.

From the living room Lisa heard the low drone of conversation. Carl rejoined the group inside. Pia, tense and angry, headed for the rear of the house. Lisa slowly climbed the stairs toward her room. At least Carl was in the drawing room—allowing extra time for Scott to make his way back unobserved.

Lisa opened her door and groped to switch on a lamp. She closed the door hastily behind her.

Scott stood with his back to a window, a look of intense excitement on his face.

"Lisa!" He strode across the room and grabbed her by the shoulders. "Lisa, Tony is here! In the closed wing! I saw him!"

TWELVE

"Scott, you saw Tony?" Lisa whispered. She trembled with anticipation, eager to hear his reassurance.

"I couldn't see his face," Scott admitted, and Lisa

could feel the tension in his hands as he clutched her shoulders. "The man was lying face down on a cot in the corner of a room, and it was dark—but he was built like Tony, tall like him."

"But we can't be sure," she said with disappointment.

"There is no doubt in my mind," Scott insisted. He released Lisa, reached into his jacket pocket for a cigarette. Lisa sat on the edge of a chair, waiting for him to continue. "I crept around to the east side of the closed wing. Right off I spied a light in a window on the second floor. You remember the vines that crawl all over that side—it was easy to make my way up the side of the house. I had to wait, of course, until the light went out. I didn't dare venture up with a light in the room."

"When the light went off, you climbed up?" Lisa picked up breathlessly. "Who was in the room?"

"I saw a man stretched out, face down on the cot in the corner. The moonlight didn't spill that far into the room. All I could see was an outline. But the man was built like Tony. One hand trailed on the floor—and it was Tony's hand. Long, strong fingers."

"How do we get him out?" Lisa asked.

"A problem," Scott conceded. "The window is barred. I wanted to call out to him, then thought better of it. I wasn't armed—in the event there was someone on the other side of the door."

"Now that we know he's a prisoner," Lisa tried, "can't we call the police in?"

"I doubt that they would take any action." Scott shook his head tiredly. "The Menotti family is respected here. The report has been spread around

town—and this I found out from tradespeople—
that Tony died of pneumonia in Paris. The police are
not going to break into the villa."

"What do you plan on doing?" Lisa tried to be
calm.

"I'll have to pick up a revolver," Scott said quietly. "Don't get upset, honey," he soothed in response
to the look of alarm that spread over her face. "It's
just for whatever possibilities might pop up." He
was silent a moment. "Lisa, I want you to cook up
a side trip first thing in the morning. Run down to
Venice for a few days."

"No." Lisa's eyes flashed. "I won't run away."

"I'll feel easier with you out of here, Lisa," Scott
insisted. "In case there's trouble. Besides, Venice is
fabulous," he went on, ignoring her head-shaking.
"What a mixture of architecture. No traffic noises,
Lisa. Picture that!" He sighed at her continued re-
fusal. "Sunsets like nothing you've ever seen. And
the masterpieces. Lisa, as an artist, you have to see
them. Tintoretto's *Paradise*, Titian's *Assumption of
the Virgin*—"

"I'm not concerned about sightseeing," Lisa interrupted firmly. "We're both here to find Tony, to help
him!"

"You could help more by keeping my mind clear
of worry," Scott pointed out, but Lisa again shook
her head. "All right, tomorrow I go into town for the
revolver. Tomorrow night I have to get into the
closed wing somehow!"

"With Carl on guard?"

"We have to gamble," Scott said. "That's why the

revolver. I'll rent a car for the rest of the week and keep it parked off the road just outside the villa. Nobody will notice."

"Carl said something about going into town on an errand late Friday afternoon. Pia will be driving the Englishwomen into Milan for their plane," Lisa said. "Carl must be making the pick-up at the apothecary shop."

"Then we're running out of time!" Scott chewed at his lip.

"Scott, I know how we can grab ourselves a chunk of safe time," Lisa said. "I had to make a date to meet Carl in town Friday. He was getting kind of obnoxious last night. If I meet him after his pick-up at the apothecary shop and keep him in town for dinner, you'll have hours to make your try! Mrs. Eddy told me they're taking a late afternoon plane, which means Pia will be away quite a while, too, also in the late afternoon. There'll be only the contessa and Rosa around. Friday is Maria's day off."

"I hate to stall another day," Scott hedged.

"Scott, it makes sense," Lisa urged. "You'll have a chance that way. It'll be less dangerous—for Tony *and* for you. Only the contessa and Rosa in the house—it's what we've been waiting for, Scott."

"I don't like you spending that much time with Carl," Scott said bluntly.

"Don't worry, darling—I can handle him."

"You're sure?" Scott appeared far from convinced.

"Sure," she insisted. "Scott, we can't take chances with Tony's safety. If anything happened to you now—" she shuddered.

"Okay, Friday afternoon late. I'll watch for Pia's departure. Carl will be in town already. Lisa, this has got to be it," Scott said desperately.

"It will be!"

They would get Tony out of whatever impossible situation he was in, Lisa thought. She was going to know her brother! Thank God for Scott. Though she would have felt the way she did about Scott even under ordinary circumstances.

"What about last night?" Scott remembered to ask. "Did you run into difficulties about the locket?"

"Not really," Lisa reported. "We decided it was too difficult to search at night. Carl promised to help me in the morning. Pia joined the search," she added. "I have the feeling that neither Pia nor the contessa entirely trusts Carl."

"They're playing a version of 'locket, locket, who's got the locket,'" Scott chuckled. "By the way, where is it?"

"I hid it in a jar of cold cream," Lisa improvised.

"Make sure you keep your doors and windows locked," Scott cautioned. "Oh, there's a new bolt on your door."

Lisa turned around to inspect her door. The shining brass hardware was a jarring note esthetically but Lisa welcomed its presence.

"When did you put it on?" she asked in astonishment.

"While you were downstairs at dinner. It took me forever, trying to be quiet about it. Whoever got into your room last night came in with a key. They won't get past the bolt," Scott promised grimly.

"Thanks," Lisa whispered softly. "Thanks for everything, Scott."

Lisa was not surprised to walk into the garden, shortly after breakfast and find Carl searching about the grounds for the missing locket. Lisa realized that she had unwittingly thrown Pia, the contessa, and Carl into pandemonium. No doubt, they suspected still another participant in this race to solve the villa's secret—and none of the three fully trust the other two.

"I have been here for over an hour, Lisa," Carl told her regretfully. "I find nothing of the locket."

"How disappointing," she said. "Do you suppose I could have lost it in town somewhere? Should I place an ad in the local paper?"

"I would not do that," Carl said almost sharply. "We will surely find it about the villa. It is just a matter of time."

Lisa sensed his impatience with himself at not finding the locket. Not to return it to her, she was sure, but to hold the locket in his hands and search for its hidden meaning. Last night she had tried without success to pry it open. Now she was convinced the locket held no tiny crevice where anything might be concealed. There has to be a message somewhere on the face of the locket.

"I suppose the others think I'm behaving like a spoiled child," Lisa apologized. "But the locket is sort of a good luck charm to me."

"A woman is allowed such a whim," Carl said indulgently. "Meanwhile, we will make a point of searching inside the villa." He rushed to help her set up her easel for the morning session of painting. "You do not forget. Tomorrow is Friday. We have a pact to meet in town. I will take you to a sumptuous place for dinner. The sort of restaurant that the tourists shun," he boasted.

"I'll be out of paints," Lisa improvised. "I'll manage to get away. Is it so unusual for an American girl to dine alone in town? I mean, from the standpoint of the other?"

"Lisel," Carl chuckled, "anything an attractive young American girl does in Italy is not unusual."

But how would he explain his own absence, Lisa wondered doubtfully? Wasn't Pia going to be suspicious? But that was Carl's problem, not hers.

As had been her custom these last few days, Lisa dutifully returned to her room after lunch for a siesta. However, she was far too restless to sleep. Marking time until tomorrow, when Scott would make the attempt to reach Tony, was going to be nerve-wracking.

Lisa strolled across to the balcony and opened up the shuttered doors to walk outside. She whistled softly, hoping that Scott would hear and come out. But there was no response. Either he was asleep or out of his room. She should have coaxed him into going swimming with her this afternoon, Lisa thought regretfully, gazing down at the stretch of white beach.

Impulsively Lisa ran to her dressing room to look for a bathing suit. She dressed swiftly, impatient now to feel the water closing in about her with its soft warmth. Sandals in one hand, she tiptoed down the stairs and raced out through the side entrance. Everyone else was asleep or resting.

Lisa was twenty feet from the edge of the beach when laughter from the other side of the high cypress hedge brought her to a halt. Her heart pounded furiously. Pia Menotti, again with Scott! A stone bench flanked the hedge on her side; Lisa sat down, her throat tight with shock.

"One never can understand you American men," Pia purred. "I tell you plainly I am interested, but *zut*, you turn away from me!"

"I'm not turning now," Scott murmured, and there was a heavy silence. Lisa's face burned.

"That was better," Pia approved. "Much better. Now you tell me, why are you really here at the villa?"

"Can't you guess?" Scott sounded amused.

"Suppose you tell me?" Pia coaxed.

"I'm here for the same reason as you," Scott said bluntly. "To latch on to a chunk of the cache."

"What do you know about it? Who are you, Scott?"

"A man looking for a fast, easy buck," Scott drawled. "Among other things."

"How do you expect to find that here?" Pia asked.

"I met Tony at an artists' ball a couple of months ago in Paris. He had been hitting the bourbon all evening—"

"I've never met you," Pia objected quickly. "I would have remembered."

"You weren't with Tony too much around that

time. We saw quite a lot of each other," Scott went
on. "Tony could be very vocal about the riches concealed here at the villa."

"Does Tony know the location?" Pia asked with
excitement. "He always said he did not!"

"Tony doesn't know—" Scott admitted, an odd
caution in his voice. "But he knew that all the painting from the villa and the family jewelry had been
hidden away by his father before the Fascists could
confiscate them."

Lisa didn't know what to believe. Was Scott really
Tony's friend, here to rescue him or not? She had
confided in him, like a lovesick little idiot. He knew
she had the locket!

"Why did you come running?" Pia challenged.
"How do you expect to find what the contessa has
been unable to find all these years?"

"Why are *you* here?" Scott countered. "Not to play
the villa manageress bit. Sweetie, you have the same
expensive tastes as old Scott here!"

"I hope Tony was lying when he said he did not
know." Pia sighed. "I was at last able to convince the
contessa that we must have the villa taken apart
stone by stone, if need be, to find what is hidden.
The contessa claims the paintings alone would bring
over a billion at auction."

Scott whistled expressively. "Tony wouldn't have
that, huh?"

"Tony is an idiot," Pia flared. "He prefers to keep
the villa intact and be without the money. I am afraid
he would refuse to sell even if we could find all that
is concealed. Tony has absurd dreams," Pia said
contemptuously, about what he can do. Did you

know he wished to welcome all kinds of starving artists into the villa?"

"You and I wouldn't be so stupid," Scott murmured hotly. "We'd know what to do with all that loot."

"When did you last see Tony?" Pia probed.

"About six weeks ago, back in Paris. Nobody knows where he disappeared. Where is he, Pia?" Scott suddenly asked.

"He is staying at a town outside of Venice," Pia said. "With his precious painting. We tell the guests I am a widow—it makes a more picturesque story. Tony and I are not *simpatico*."

"How did you get into the act with the contessa?" Scott wanted to know. "You must have had to buy your way in somehow."

"The contessa hopes I will have influence with Tony. She still suspects Tony knows the secret hiding place."

"He was a child during the war," Scott reminded her.

"He was ten when his father died," Pia flashed back, "and they were deeply attached. There was nothing his father would not tell him. He even had Tony running errands for the partisans. But Tony insists he does not know where the cache is."

"I'd believe him," Scott said. "There has to be another angle."

"What?" Pia demanded.

"The waiter down at the restaurant—the one who tried to nab Lisa Kirby's locket," Scott began cautiously.

"Do you know everything?" Pia asked in astonishment.

"What about the locket?"

"I do not know why I tell you this," Pia stalled.

"Because this pie is big enough to cut into another wedge," Scott said briskly. "What about Lisa Kirby's locket?"

"The waiter came to tell us he knows the locket. He could not believe his eyes when he saw it on the Kirby girl. The waiter was a partisan fighting with Tony's father during the war. He knows Mario Menotti concealed the villa treasures, then had the locket made and inscribed in some fashion with the secret hiding place. It is all there, somewhere in the locket! The waiter's brother, who has been dead two years now, made the locket. It was *not* made for the contessa." Irony entered her voice.

"You have it, of course," Scott said coolly.

"No!" Pia shot back, startled. Her dark eyes narrowed. "Can it be that the wide-eyed Miss Kirby is not so wide-eyed after all? Scott, she knows about the locket! She must have it! She is playing some game with us—this business of losing it!"

Lisa raced back to the house. She was sick at heart and frightened. She was utterly alone in a villa of terror. Was Tony in that other closed wing as Scott had claimed—or in Venice? Was that just another of Scott's lies, conjured up to deceive her? Was that all she had heard from Scott all this time? Lies, lies, lies.

THIRTEEN

Lisa took a side path that led to the west terrace; the glass doors would be open. She was trembling inside, fighting back tears of disappointment and humiliation. How had she allowed herself to fall for Scott Anderson's elaborate line. No wonder he kept asking where she hid the locket! He was after it himself!

Lisa tiptoed towards the staircase, but paused for a moment when she heard the contessa's voice in the rear of the house.

"If you lie to me, Maria, it will be bad with you," the contessa shouted. "Where is the American girl's locket?"

"I told you," Maria sobbed indignantly. "I never see the locket. I never take what is not mine!"

"Then who has taken it?" the contessa asked in quiet fury. "Where has it disappeared?"

Lisa hurried upstairs, impatient to be able to sit down and think about tomorrow. Should she leave with Mrs. Eddy and her friends? She reached her door, opened it and walked inside. Lock the bolt, she reminded herself. Suddenly, with sickening comprehension she realized how clever Scott had been . . . Lock out the others while he had free rein to search her room!

Lisa crossed to the dressing room; her eyes settled on a massive fruitwood chest that stood against one wall. She struggled to move the chest against the hidden panel.

The chest was unwieldy, but gradually it began to move along the polished floor. She would be able to manage it, Lisa decided in relief. No one would enter her room tonight. Tomorrow she must make a decision before the others left. But would they—the contessa, Pia, even Scott—permit her to leave when the locket was unaccounted for? Her locker held the ultimate secret to the treasure hidden somewhere within the villa walls.

Lisa lay across the bed struggling for calm. How could she have been so wrong about a man, the way she was wrong about Scott? She had been on the point of entrusting the locket to Scott. With the locket Scott would be in complete command—he could call all the plays.

A short time later, Lisa went into the dressing room to change from her bathing suit into a duster. She loved the cotton duster with its blend of rich blues and greens. Its flowing fullness from shoulder to knee gave her a sense of floating. Her mother had given it to her for her birthday over a year ago. Nineteen had been a glorious year, Lisa thought wistfully. With twenty came grief.

Lisa opened an enormous jar of cold cream that sat on a shelf. She had utilized her lie to Scott; in the depths of the cold cream nestled her locket, in a thick protective wrapping. After this afternoon the locket would never leave her person! She unwrapped it, gazed in perplexity at its familiar pattern and turned it over to peruse the quotation from Dante on the back. The quotation! In some way, the quotation must hold the secret of the hiding place.

In the next room Lisa heard sounds of activity, then a gentle tapping on the panel. She stiffened, waiting for sounds of force. He couldn't push through that heavy fruitwood chest without help. In a few moments the knocking was abandoned. Lisa heard no effort to push through the panel.

Let Scott sit in his room and believe she was asleep. She would keep clear of him tonight. Miss King was forever trying to inveigle someone into a chess game before dinner. Tonight Lisa would accept; there would be no opportunity for Scott to force himself upon her.

If she were sensible, Lisa told herself, she would ride into Milan tomorrow afternoon when Pia drove the women to the airport. She would go with her passport, her visa, her health certificate, and her American Express checks—and take the first plane out of Milan that was bound for New York. Or a train to Venice—she had no possible way of knowing that Tony was actually here. Pia could have been the one telling the truth. Tony could be in Venice with his artist friends. She could hardly blame him for wanting to be away from his wife and his stepmother!

Lisa waited until she heard Miss King and Mrs. Eddy heading down the stairs before leaving her room. For the last twenty minutes Scott had been at the typewriter, keeping up the writer's pretense. For whom? Pia knew it was a lie! Quickly, she darted from her room, eager to join the two women ahead of her.

"Miss King," she called gaily, "if you're in a chess mood tonight, you have a partner."

Lisa and Miss King settled themselves over a chessboard in a far corner of the room. Lisa was glad of a need to concentrate on the game. From the corner of her eye she saw that Scott had joined the before-dinner group. She was conscious of the repeated quizzical glances he shot in her direction.

A few moments before Rosa was scheduled to announce dinner, Carl strolled into the drawing room. He carried a bottle of champagne, which he took immediately to Pia. Lisa realized that tonight was to be a festive dinner, in honor of the guests who were leaving.

Rosa's dinner was a sumptuous feast that brought forth exclamations of delight from everyone at the table. But despite the gourmet banquet, the champagne, the convivial conversation, Lisa felt an undercurrent of tension.

"No signs yet of your locket, Miss Kirby?" the contessa inquired with a display of solicitude.

"None at all," Lisa sighed.

For a second, Lisa's eyes met Scott's. The others—Mrs. Eddy, Miss King, even Pia—seemed to be aware that she was avoiding Scott. No doubt Mrs. Eddy and Miss King were romantically dreaming up a lover's quarrel.

"I have arranged for entertainment for this evening," the contessa announced with a regal smile as they prepared to go into the drawing room for coffee. "A young couple from a nearby village will sing folk songs for us. I believe you will find this enjoyable."

"What a lovely thought," Miss King bubbled ec-statically.

Pia attached herself to Scott with an air of pos-sessiveness. Carl was instantly beside Lisa.

The young man and young woman were patiently awaiting their orders. The girl was seated with the guitar across her lap. The man hovered over her af-fectionately. They are in love, Lisa thought, touched by their honesty.

The group settled down in the drawing room to lis-ten to the entertainment while Maria bustled about serving coffee. Lisa felt the faint pressure of Carl's fingers on her shoulder as he leaned near her in the semi-darkness. The rich, plaintive voices of the two singers filled the room.

"Let us listen from the terrace," Carl coaxed after a few moments. "It is such a beautiful night."

Wordlessly, Lisa rose from her chair and moved away on tiptoe. A faint stirring at the other side of the room told her that Scott was aware of her move-ment. Let him be annoyed!

"We're terribly rude," Lisa whispered when they were safely outside. Carl was right, though; it was a glorious night.

"Not really rude," he reassured her. "We are en-joying the music out here."

"It's lovely," Lisa said, disconcerted by his close-ness.

"Lisel," he said gently. "I think it is now time for some truths. You have guessed I am not what I appear—"

"I gathered," Lisa said.

"I am a German, yes," he smiled. "I spent two years at Buchenwald, as a political prisoner," he emphasized. "Now I am an intelligence agent for the Italian government."

"You are here on an assignment?" Lisa stared in astonishment.

"The Italian government is convinced there are treasures hidden away at the villa that are the property of the government. I have been ordered to find them. In Paris I deliberately made the acquaintance of Pia Menotti. It was not difficult."

"I'm sure of that," Lisa said.

"I came here hoping to find some lead that would enable the government to step in. Mr. Anderson was a surprise element. He is, I am quite confident, an adventurer, after the cache, also."

"Why do you think that?" Lisa asked.

"He gives himself away." In the moonlight Lisa could see the eloquent shrug of his shoulders. "In my business a man learns to recognize these things. Perhaps he knew Pia's husband, heard him boasting about the treasures."

"What about her husband?" Lisa asked breathlessly. "Where is he?"

"We have lost our trail on Tony Menotti. He disappeared in Paris, some weeks ago."

"Carl," Lisa said desperately, "could Tony be here, at the villa?"

"Impossible." Carl stared at her. "Are you a friend of Tony's? Are you here at the Villa on his behalf?"

"He's my half-brother," Lisa whispered, throwing caution aside. "That's why I'm here, Carl. To find Tony."

"You must not let the others know!" Carl said.

His gaze swept toward the open door, but the sound of their voices was drowned out by the singing. "Lisa, I have reason to believe your locket holds the secret to the location of the cache. Where is it?"

"But you know I lost it," Lisa stammered. "All of a sudden it was gone." She couldn't bring herself to admit that she carried the locket next to her skin.

"Then it was stolen from your room." His eyes narrowed.

"I could have lost it," she persisted uneasily.

"Lisa, I need your help. We must find your locket!"

"What about Tony?" Lisa searched his face anxiously. "Carl, is Tony in some kind of trouble with the government?"

"Not if the paintings are recovered. But as I told you, our men have lost their trail on Tony. He disappeared into nothing." Carl snapped his fingers. "Like that."

"How do we go about finding the locket?" Lisa asked. Should she tell Carl? He had leveled with her. He admitted he was an agent of the Italian government. But could she believe him? After Scott, could she believe anyone?

"The first step is to search your room. If you permit this," Carl said slowly, with unfamiliar formality, "we would be most grateful. It is possible that you accidentally dropped it somewhere," he conceded. "If not, then we must suspect the others in the villa."

"Tomorrow afternoon, during the siesta hour?" Lisa offered after a moment.

"Before I leave for my business in town." His eyes

held hers, warm with anticipation. "You do not forget, we have a meeting arranged."

"I remember," she smiled, fighting against her feeling of panic. "Carl, perhaps I should tell you. Someone broke into my room—night before last. A woman. I couldn't see who it was. She came at me with a pillow but I ran away when Scott came into my room. There's a secret panel in my dressing room that backs Scott's—she escaped through that while he was with me."

"Pia!" Some of the brutal anger Lisa remembered in Carl from that first encounter showed through now. "She is determined!"

"But last night in the garden," Lisa reminded him, "she was afraid you would find the locket and cut her out."

"It could have been a pretense," Carl said contemptuously. "These people trust no one because they know themselves."

"What is there about the locket that's so important?" Lisa tried. "There's no secret compartment, nothing like that!"

"The inscription on the back," Carl explained, and Lisa felt a surge of excitement that he had confirmed her own conclusions. "It is a kind of code. If I can get it to the government code offices, they will be able to break it in an hour."

"We'd better get back inside," Lisa said. "The others will notice."

Scott stood just inside the opened glass doors. His face was drawn tightly. Hanging onto his arm was Pia Menotti, her eyes flashing dangerously.

In her room Lisa lay sleepless, pondering Carl Obermann's revelation about himself. Before she committed herself fully to Carl, she would have to know that he wasn't lying to her. How would she do that? The American Consulate in Milan. They were so solicitous of young American girls on the loose in Italy. She could hint at an affair and ask them to check out Carl.

With a sigh of relief at having arrived at a course of action, Lisa turned over on one side determined to sleep. Once again she heard the furtive tapping in her dressing room. Lisa lay motionless, ignoring the tapping. Let the enterprising Mr. Scott Anderson figure that out!

Moments later, Lisa heard a door opening down the corridor. There was a scraping sound, like something being slipped beneath her door. She sat up and spied a scrap of white just inside her door. She picked it up.

"Lisa, I must talk to you. About Tony. Open up or I'll cause a rumpus right out here!" Scott had scrawled. He probably meant it, about starting a rumpus, she thought uneasily.

"Wait," she whispered. She opened the door a few inches. "What is it, Scott?"

"I can't talk out here in the hall," he said impatiently.

Lisa pulled the door open, waited for him to enter and shut it behind him.

"What's the matter with you, you little character?" Scott demanded. "You've been avoiding me all evening."

"Is that why you've forced your way in here?" she asked.

"It was for this," Scott said quietly, holding his hand out palm up.

Lisa looked doubtfully at the key in Scott's hand. "What is it?"

"I've finally got through to Rosa. She took this from the contessa's room. You'll have to go into town first thing in the morning—the town to the west, where you've never been seen. Have a copy of the key made and bring it back before noon," he explained. "Rosa has to have it back before the contessa wakes up."

Lisa took the key between slim fingers. "What is it for?"

"It's the key to the room in the closed wing where they're keeping Tony prisoner!"

"I can say I have to go in to buy brushes," Lisa improvised uncertainly. "That'll cover." Should she go along with this? Was it a ruse to get her away from the villa?

"I can't take a chance on going in myself," Scott said. "It'll be easier for you to get away with it. Be sure you're back at the villa well before noon. Rosa's a nervous wreck." He headed for her dressing room.

"Where are you going?" Lisa asked quickly.

"The short cut," Scott grinned, looking surprised.

"Maria noticed that the tapestry was pushed aside this afternoon," Lisa stammered. "I had to ask her to help me put the chest against it."

Why did Scott look at her as though he had never seen her before? Hadn't he been handing her nothing but a pack of lies these past weeks? Tomorrow, some-

how, she must find out where the truth lay. With
Scott? With Carl? The real truth—not what she preferred to believe was the truth. She would have Scott's
key made all right, in Milan . . . where she could
also check with the American Consulate.

FOURTEEN

Lisa was already dressed when she heard a timid
knock at her door.

"Who is it?" she asked cautiously, her fingers on
the locked bolt.

"Rosa." Her voice was barely a whisper.

Lisa slid the bolt free and pulled open the door.
Rosa stood there with the breakfast tray, her eyes
lowered, fearful of meeting Lisa's.

"Signor Anderson say you like breakfast early."
Rosa made it sound like a prepared speech. Her
hands were unsteady on the tray.

"Thank you, Rosa," Lisa said softly. Was Rosa
working with Scott . . . had she in reality provided
the key that would give Tony his freedom? It was impossible to interpret Rosa's furtive behavior. Well
. . . in a matter of hours, she would *know*.

"You eat outdoors," Rosa said. "*Multo bello*. The
birds, the sunshine—" Rosa was talking to mask her
nervousness.

"It's a beautiful day," Lisa agreed.

"*Signorina*," Rosa said worriedly. "Take care."

Before Lisa could reply, Rosa turned and scurried to the door.

"Rosa," Lisa called and walked swiftly to the door.

"*Si, Signorina?*" Rosa's eyes looked frightened as she stood stock still in the corridor.

"I've ruined all my paint brushes—I'm going into town to shop . . . if anyone should ask."

"*Si, Signorina,*" Rosa bobbed her head in comprehension, then trundled on down the stairs.

Lisa ate quickly. It was barely eight o'clock; if she hurried, she could catch the early bus into Milan. If Scott were leveling with her, it was urgent that she be back with the key before the contessa awakened. She would be pressed for time.

As Lisa walked down the path to the gates, she tried to frame in her mind the words to use at the American Consulate. Even if she had to play a neurotic, hysterical American girl in the midst of a wild love affair, she would do it. She had to be sure of Carl before she returned to the Villa.

If Carl were an agent for the Italian government, then Tony must be somewhere in Venice. But if Carl were lying—and this key that rested in her purse was truly the road to Tony's release, then there was no time to lose. This was Friday! This afternoon, late, Carl was going into town to pick up the package at the apothecary. This was Maria's day off; the English guests were flying to Naples. The stage was set for whatever terrible plan the others might harbor for Tony's future.

The bus arrived and she boarded it. There was much good-humored grumbling among the passengers because the bus was running ten minutes behind schedule. Even so, they would arrive in Milan not much past nine. She would go into a shop to have the key made and then present herself at the American Consulate. Please, she prayed silently, none of those lengthy delays one sometimes encountered at consulate offices. Not today!

The bus rattled finally to its destination in Milan. For the first time Lisa realized how irrational her behavior must have appeared to those at the villa. An American girl, on her first trip to Italy, and she had been content to stay within the villa when Leonardo Da Vinci's "The Last Supper" was on a wall of the convent of Santa Maria delle Grazie right here in Milan! And the fabulous collection of Da Vinci drawings on exhibit in the Palazzo de Brera. And Michelangelo's "Pieta" on view in the Castello Sforzesco.

The excitement that would grip any American artist within a stone's throw of such historic treasures now enveloped Lisa. That passion for museums that her mother had encouraged returned. She fondly recalled the countless Sundays and holidays in New York they had spent wandering through the Metropolitan, the Whitney and the Museum of Modern Art. No doubt, her mother's great love of art had been born of those months when she and Mario Menotti had walked the streets of Milan, sharing its pleasures. Those few short months when they had made love and planned for a future together that was never to be.

Lisa abandoned the pretext of an American who spoke no Italian. She asked, and was directed to a shop where keys might be made in a matter of minutes. It would be futile to present herself at the American Consulate before nine-thirty. She waited for the key to be made, exchanging polite small talk with the man in the shop. He complimented her on her Italian and was interested in her reasons for being in Italy. Lisa deliberately avoided any mention of the Villa Como, though in a city the size of Milan there was little chance that the Menotti name would lift an eyebrow.

By the time she arrived, the American Consulate was coming slowly to life. She waited in the reception room while the less-exalted members of the staff began to pick up the daily threads of their jobs. She fretted nervously. Finally, the girl at the desk signalled for her to go inside. She found herself face to face with a tall, kindly aide. "Please sit down, Miss Kirby," he smiled, intent on putting her at her ease.

Lisa began to explain the purpose of her visit. He had heard this story before, Lisa guessed. She determinedly ploughed ahead, pretending to be an impulsive young American girl in the midst of an hectic affair with an Italian.

"I thought," Lisa stammered, "if there were some way to be sure about Carl. I know sometimes things are different from what they appear on the surface. Could you check it out for me, see if he is really an intelligence agent for the Italian government?"

"We will make some discreet inquiries," the official promised politely.

"I have to know today!" Lisa said insistently, color burning in her cheeks. "Before I go back to the villa!"

"That's almost asking the impossible," he said.

"Then I'll have to believe him," Lisa brazened it

out. "You see, Carl plans to fly to Spain tonight."

"Miss Kirby, you're very young," he hesitated unhappily. "Surely you should give this deeper consideration. An older man, a foreigner—all very glamorous away from home—" he gestured eloquently.

"Find out if he's telling me the truth," Lisa pleaded.

He squinted in thought. "I'll see what I can find out, Miss Kirby," he promised. "Can you be back at the Consulate in one hour?"

"I'll be back," Lisa promised. An hour . . . it was already ten o'clock. She would just about make it to the villa before the deadline! It would be unthinkable to involve Rosa by not getting the key back in time.

Lisa strolled to the Piazza della Scala and inspected the exterior of the La Scala Opera House, now dark until winter. She tried futilely to become involved in the sightseeing. She left the Piazza to visit the Galleria Vittorio Emanuele. At the covered shopping arcade she bought a batch of postcards to send to friends back in New York. At the last moment, when it was almost time to return to the Consulate, she remembered to stop into an art supplies shop for paint brushes.

When she returned to the Consulate, the girl at the reception desk greeted her expectantly.

"You are to go right inside, Miss Kirby."

The aide was seated behind his desk, a look of apprehension on his face.

"Miss Kirby, I can only urge you to break off any alliance you may have with this Carl Obermann. He is in no way affiliated with the Italian government.

We have checked further into files. Carl Obermann was tried as a Nazi war criminal; he served time in prison for his activities at Buchenwald. He was notorious for his work in inducing insanity in prisoners!"

The bus was interminably slow on its route back to the villa. Lisa sat at the edge of her seat, nervous at the delay. There were few passengers on the return trip, but at each stop the driver launched into avid conversation that sapped up additional time. Why didn't he hurry? Did schedules mean nothing on these bus lines?

Perspiration broke out on her forehead. Every moment counted now—and the driver had to discuss the feeding schedule of his eleventh child with the old woman now boarding the bus!

Finally, the bus stopped at the villa gates. Twenty minutes to twelve! She hoped the contessa would not deviate from her normal schedule of arising at noon. Lisa raced up the path to the villa.

She entered the villa from the side terrace and hurried up the stairs. Then she stopped dead because from the far end of the corridor, from the contessa's personal suite, came a furious voice pouring out invectives. The contessa was awake! The contessa was berating Rosa for something—no doubt the missing key. Lisa stiffened as she heard a sharp slap. Rosa broke into loud sobbing.

Lisa moved swiftly to Scott's door and knocked softly. He opened it immediately and pulled her inside.

"Scott, trouble," she whispered. "The contessa is

awake. She knows the key is missing! She's screaming at Rosa now!"

"Give the copy to me," he ordered. "Go back to your room and stay there! Oh, the original key," he said. "We'll have to hide it for now." His eyes swept the room. "Under the rug, there in the corner." He crossed to a chest and took a revolver from beneath a pile of clothing.He checked the revolver, then concealed it beneath his jacket. "Lisa," his hand gripped her arm for a moment. "Go to your room and lock it. Don't open the door for anyone, do you understand? Stay in your room!"

"Let me go with you," Lisa pleaded.

"No!" Scott said firmly. "I have the car stashed away beside the villa wall. I must get Tony out of the house and into the car. Go to your room, Lisa," he insisted, already at the door, waiting for her to follow.

Lisa allowed Scott to walk her to her room. Then she heard him making his way down the stairs. Where was Pia, Lisa worried? Where was Carl Obermann? What good would the revolver be against those two? They would surely be armed themselves!

She waited for a few moments, uncertain about what to do. She couldn't stay here, not when Scott was risking his life for Tony. She opened the door and tiptoed to the stairs. A door opened noisily above her. Lisa leaned back against the wall, grateful for the shadows.

"Pia! Pia, come up here at once!" the contessa called imperiously.

"What is it?" Pia called from below after a moment.

"You will please come up here instantly," the contessa ordered.

Caught between the two, Lisa decided to walk down the stairs. Pia was ascending the stairs now, a look of sulky vexation on her face.

"Good morning," Lisa nodded.

"Good morning, Miss Kirby." Pia swept past her impatiently.

With Pia out of sight, Lisa picked up speed, anxious to catch up with Scott. She raced through the foyer to the front entrance, her eyes worriedly scanning the scenery for a sign of Carl.

She knew Carl Obermann would stop at nothing if he found Scott and Lisa in his way. At least she knew that the locket's secret lay in the inscription on the back. And that the locket rested at this moment in safety, close to her heart. But if Carl, Pia, and the contessa thought clearly, they would soon guess that the locket remained with her! And her life would mean nothing.

As she raced through the neat avenue of clipped cypress, Lisa thought she heard footsteps at the front of the house. She stopped for a moment to see who it was.

It was Rosa, half-walking, half-running toward the gates. At least nothing would happen to Rosa, Lisa thought with relief. She could account for Pia and the contessa, but where was Carl?

She hurried on until she caught sight of Scott. He was standing at a side door swearing under his breath.

"Scott," she whispered urgently.

He spun around. "Lisa, what are you doing here?"

"I have to help," she insisted, breathless from her run.

"Stand back!" Scott lunged toward the door; the lock gave way. He reached inside his jacket for the revolver. "Let's go."

They entered the murky corridor of the closed wing—Scott in the lead, Lisa close behind him. Lisa cast terrified glances behind them regularly as they advanced toward a wide staircase. Scott caught his toe in the torn carpet and almost fell. Lisa gasped, watching him struggle to regain his balance.

"I saw the light on this floor," Scott whispered.

Lisa fought down panic. Where was Carl? Hiding behind what door?

They crept down the corridor. Scott tried to place the room in which he had seen the man they believed to be Tony.

"Let's try this one," Scott said tensely. He tried the key in the lock.

"Wrong door?" Lisa asked after a moment.

"Wait," he ordered brusquely, struggling with the key in his left hand, the revolver firmly grasped in his right.

"Let me," Lisa ordered, and moved forward to try the large key in the ancient lock.

The lock turned over. Lisa pushed the door open. The room inside was partially in shadows, though here and there the noonday sun shone through the barred window. Scott shot past her and leaned over the man on the cot. He was a handsome, dark-haired young man of about thirty, with the beautifully regular features of the boy in the portrait. Scott didn't have to tell Lisa. This was Tony Menotti! This was her brother!

"Tony," Scott whispered. "Tony, for God's sake!"

Scott shook him gently by the shoulders, repeating his name over and over.

"He must be drugged," Lisa whispered in alarm. "Scott, how will we get him out of here?"

"We have to somehow," Scott said. "Tony!"

Tony began to mumble. His blue eyes, strikingly like Lisa's, were open now, trying to cope with the situation.

"Scott," he murmured tiredly. "Thought you'd never come!"

"Tony, we have to get out of here," Scott said urgently, trying to get him into a sitting position.

"Rosa sent the cable," Tony felt impelled to explain. "Poor old girl—scared to death—but sent cable . . . Her brother is a waiter . . . who knew my father. He is in with the others to take over the Menotti treasures . . . Big joke," Tony chuckled groggily. "Never find without the locket . . ."

"We have the locket!" Lisa came forward.

"Who's the girl?" Tony stiffened, shook his head as though to clear it.

"Your sister, you lucky chump," Scott said as he dragged Tony to his feet.

"You're crazy." Tony shook his head and swayed dizzily. "They keep shooting me with needles—"

"No more," Scott promised. "But let's get you out of here."

"What about the locket?" Tony stared at Lisa, not fully comprehending yet.

"I have it," she whispered. "The others don't know —I pretended to lose it about the grounds. Tony, Eloise Kirby was my mother—the American nurse!"

"The beautiful American," Tony whispered. "They were so in love." His eyes searched Lisa's face. "Meo Dio, the Menotti look," he confirmed incredulously.

"Mother had the locket all these years, Tony."

"The secret is on the back of the locket," Tony began.

"In the Dante quotation," Lisa confirmed.

Tony took an experimental step under Scott's guidance. He was big. It would be hard for Scott to carry him all the way to the car. And he was still so unsteady on his feet.

"Inscription is not accurate," Tony managed an ironic smile. "I remember my father told me, all those years ago—I was not yet ten. Father knew Dante like the Bible, but he misquoted. He had words deliberately omitted. If we use every fourth word, then go back and use every second word, we will have the key to where everything lies buried."

"Wait a moment," Lisa said. Turning away from the two men, she fumbled beneath her jacket to free the locket. "The locket, Tony." She held it toward him. In reality it belonged to both of them.

"It was designed for the woman we hoped some day would be my mother," Tony said, his voice deep with emotion. "The American nurse whom my father loved, and who for a little while lived in the villa and brought us such happiness."

"You take it for now, Scott," Tony said.

"We will take it," a voice snapped out bitingly. A guttural German voice.

Lisa, eyes wide with shock, swung about to face Carl Obermann. He stood there, the Luger in his hand, a look of victory on his face. Pia and the contessa stood behind him.

"Thank you, Tony," the contessa said with a mocking smile. "You have saved us much decoding time."

"You vile witch!" Tony lunged towards the contessa. "You desecrated my father's memory! With your Fascist and your Nazi officers!"

Scott caught him and eased him back on to the cot.

"It is a shame you Americans must be so curious," Carl said. "So impulsive and emotional."

"Take them down below," Pia said impatiently. "We have no need for this conversation. There is much to be done."

"Relax, Pia," Carl said. "The Englishwomen leave this afternoon. Maria is off. We will take care of everything tonight. Meanwhile, it is time for Tony's injection." Carl drew Pia directly in front of himself, and placed the Luger in her right hand.

Lisa watched Carl reach inside his jacket. First, he took out a case that held a hypodermic needle, then a small bottle.

"No!" Lisa gasped as Carl moved toward Tony. She lunged at Carl, battling as Scott restrained her. "Let me go, Scott!"

"How loyal," the contessa drawled. "How American!"

"Is this how it was done at Buchenwald?" Scott questioned. "Or have you improved on your technique since those days?"

"Carl knows his business," Pia said. "When you are committed, Tony, we will send you paints and brushes twice every year."

"I doubt that Signor Menotti will be committed!" an unfamiliar Italian voice shouted. "We have heard enough!"

Pia screamed as a cluster of Italian police swarmed into the room from the shadowed corridors.

Pia's eyes darted about in frenzy; then she aimed the Luger at the police officer barking out orders.

"Watch it!" Scott yelled as he threw himself at Pia.

The Luger went off. The shot was wild, and the bullet imbedded itself in a wall. Two of the invading police grabbed Pia's wrists while she struggled and swore. Tony swayed on his feet, an arm protectively about Lisa. Carl and the contessa were marched out of the room at gunpoint.

"Signor Menotti," the police officer said, "we are happy to see you are alive. Our town honors the memory of your dead father. We hope you will stay now at the Villa Como."

"I will be here, thank you," Tony managed, smiling faintly.

Lisa and Scott walked Tony slowly down the stairs to the floor below and out toward the door. The three of them emerged into the sunlight. The weeks of terror were over, Lisa thought with grateful relief. She had found her brother. Together, they would find the treasures of the Villa Como. And she had found Scott Anderson.

They could see the police herding their quarry into the cars waiting at the villa entrance. Mrs. Eddy was scurrying past the police, with the Misses King and Lounsbury right behind her.

"Thank heaven you are all right!" Mrs. Eddy called breathlessly as she approached them.

"This is my brother Tony," Lisa said proudly. "Scott and I both came here to find him. He was being held a prisoner." They sat Tony on a bench.

"Rosa told us to call the police," Mrs. Eddy reported. "We did so instantly!" Her eyes darted from one to the other of the trio in pleasurable excitement. "Nobody back home will ever believe us when we tell them all that happened while we were here at the villa!"

"Is everything all right now, Miss Kirby?" Miss King asked. "I mean—with Mr. Anderson and you?" Her gaze rested happily, first on Lisa, then on Scott.

"Nothing could be better," Scott grinned, pressing Lisa's slender hand. "Of course, there can't be a wedding at the Villa Como until my future brother-in-law is completely recovered."

"You wire us," Mrs. Eddy said, "and we will fly straight back from Naples. Can you imagine?" she bubbled effervescently, turning to the Misses King and Lounsbury, "when we go back to our school in September, they simply won't believe us when we tell them about the Villa Como. They'll insist we have made up every shred of what's happened!"

Lisa and Scott were in no position to comment. They were engaged in very personal consultation.

"I don't really mind too much if we miss Puccini's home," Miss King confided, viewing the scene with approval. "After all, he's been dead for years."